It's going to be an action-packed year. . . .

I looked at my new friends Emily and Lexie. I'd only met them a few hours ago and already they were talking about getting together for sleepovers. I couldn't believe how lucky I was. I'd been scared that I wouldn't make any friends here at all. And now I had two great friends to hang out with.

"You know what?" Lexie said. "This school year is going to be fun after all. I thought it was going to be a real downer after getting back from L.A., but now I'm looking forward to it."

"Me, too," Emily said. Her face was all bright and sparkling again. "You don't know how great it is to be at a real school with real people after five years of Pee Wee Pugh and his gross friends making animal noises and pulling my braids."

An hour earlier I had been sitting thinking how much I missed my old friends and my old school and how I'd never fit in here. But now I realized that there was a lot to look forward to. Whatever happened this year, with Emily and Lexie around it wouldn't be boring.

"It's going to be totally fun," I said.

Check out the fantastic sleepover tips in the back of this book!

TGIF!

Sleepover Madness

JANET QUIN-HARKIN

A MINSTREL® BOOK

Published by POCKET BOOKS

New York   London   Toronto   Sydney   Tokyo   Singapore

This book is a work of fiction. Names, characters, places, and incidents are either products of the author's imagination or are used fictitiously. Any resemblance to actual events or locales or persons, living or dead, is entirely coincidental.

A MINSTREL PAPERBACK *Original*

A Minstrel Book published by
POCKET BOOKS, a division of Simon & Schuster Inc.
1230 Avenue of the Americas, New York, NY 10020

Produced by Daniel Weiss Associates, Inc., New York

Copyright © 1995 by Daniel Weiss Associates, Inc., and Janet Quin-Harkin
Cover art copyright © 1995 by Daniel Weiss Associates, Inc.

ISBN: 0-671-51017-7

First Minstrel Books printing September 1995

10 9 8 7 6 5 4 3 2 1

A MINSTREL BOOK and colophon are registered trademarks of Simon & Schuster Inc.

Printed in the U.S.A.

ONE

"Mom, I don't feel so good."

I clutched the kitchen door for support. I was finding it hard to breathe, and the room was swaying around me.

My family was in the middle of breakfast. Dad had a cup of coffee in one hand and his briefcase in the other. My brother, Tom, was shoveling pancakes into his face as fast as my mother could cook them. He's fourteen and he can eat more food than anybody I've ever seen. He's totally gross in other ways, too, and he's turning into the biggest pain in the world—but more about him later.

Everybody looked up.

"My stomach hurts real bad."

"Really bad. *Really* is an adverb," said my English-expert sister, Christine. She went back to chopping a humongous pile of vegetables. I wondered if we'd gotten a zoo and nobody had told me, but I was feeling too weak to ask.

"Really bad," I snapped. "Who cares how I say it? My stomach hurts a lot."

1

"Nice try," Tom said, spluttering into his pancakes with that phony laugh of his, "but it won't work. I used to pull that stunt all the time. Mom never fell for it."

"You don't understand," I wailed, ignoring Tom. "My stomach really does hurt me, Mom. And I can't breathe. It has to be a stomach flu, or maybe my appendix is about to burst."

Mom looked up from pouring orange juice with that patient, annoying smile of hers. "It's called first-day-of-school nerves, Kaitlin, dear," she said in her clipped British accent. "It's quite understandable. Having to go to a new school is hard for anyone."

"Not me," Tom said. "I'm going to be an eighth grader, big man on campus, king of the hill, top of the heap. I'm going to kick butt."

"Tom, I don't want to hear that sort of talk again," my mother said.

My dad frowned in Tom's direction. "You're not going to school to kick butt. You're going to get good grades." He gave my mom a quick peck on the cheek and headed for the front door. "Have a good day at school, kids," he called.

"No problem," Christine muttered.

I looked at Christine in surprise. She sure was doing a lot of chopping. Up and down, chop, chop, chop her hands were going, and celery was flying in all directions.

"Are you nervous about going to a new school, too, Christine?" I asked her.

"Nervous? Who said anything about nervous?" she snapped, and went on chopping. I was amazed. She *was* nervous. I'd always thought of her as Ms. Supercool, student council member and debate team whiz.

Mom must have noticed it, too. "Christine, that's an awful lot of vegetables for one lunch," she said. "Or are you planning to feed the entire junior class?"

"Mom, you know I'm a vegetarian now," Christine said. "And I'll probably never find my way to the cafeteria, so I have to be prepared."

"Oh, poor baby, she'll get lost in the big new scary high school," Tom said.

"Shut up, dog breath. Mom, make him shut up," Christine said. She sounded close to tears.

"Tom, finish your breakfast and make your lunch, or you'll miss the bus." Mom's voice was firm.

"Make my lunch? You want me to make my own lunch?"

"Who was just boasting about being king of the hill? I'd say you were old enough to make your own lunch," Mom said smoothly. She went over to the coffeepot and poured herself a cup.

"That's women's work," he muttered as he got to his feet.

"What did you say?" Mom demanded.

"Nothing," Tom growled. He knows better than to say stuff like that to our mom, who belongs to lots of women's organizations. "You should have warned me. I wanted to ride my bike to school. If I have to make my lunch, I won't have time."

"I wanted you to go on the bus anyway. Kaitlin needs you to look after her on the first day. You have to make sure she gets to the right classroom. Middle

3

school is a whole new experience for her. I'm trusting you to keep an eye out for her, Tom."

"Good luck," Christine muttered, giving me a grin. "Kaitlin will be lucky if she even gets as far as the bus stop with him taking care of her."

"Does that mean I have to go to school?" I asked. I couldn't understand how they could be discussing me so calmly while I was clutching the doorframe with my appendix about to explode. "You're not going to take me to the doctor?"

"No, Kaitlin, I'm not," Mom said. "And if you don't get a move on, you'll be sitting on that bus in your fuzzy bathrobe."

"Fine!" I exclaimed. "If I'm very infectious and the whole sixth grade comes down with stomach flu, it will be your fault."

My mother smiled. "Kaitlin, you'll be fine as soon as you get on the bus and meet people. Trust me."

"I might feel better if I didn't have to wear that dumb skirt," I said. "It's very tight around the waist."

"Kaitlin, we've been through all this before," Mom said. She didn't sound so calm and understanding now. "I like my children to be properly dressed, especially on the first day of school. First impressions are very important, you know."

"Yeah, and the first impression of me will be that I'm a geek," I growled.

"Nonsense. Plaid kilts are very fashionable this year. I showed you those pictures in the fashion magazines."

"Fashionable for old people, maybe. Eleven-year-olds don't read those magazines."

"You can't win with her, you know," Christine said to me as she shoved vegetables into a Zip-loc bag. "I had to go to school for years looking like the world's youngest secretary. Now it's your turn."

I stomped back up the stairs. Christine was right. There was no use arguing with Mom. She is the most stubborn, annoying person in the world. We'd had this big fight in the store. I wanted overalls, and she wanted the pleated plaid skirt. Guess who won? "Overalls?" she said. "Why would you want to look as if you've just finished milking the cows?" It's no use trying to explain to her, because she's still living in the Stone Age. If she had her way, every school would have uniforms like the one she had to wear when she was a kid in England. So she made me get the next best thing. She even had me believing that it was fashionable. I shuddered as I looked at myself in the mirror.

My hair was flyaway and more red than blond, and there was no way I could hide the face of a million freckles. I was stuck with looking like the geek of the month. That sure wouldn't help me make friends on my first day. What if they all laughed at me? I knew that a lot of farm kids went to our school. I'd bet they all wore jeans every day. I'd bet they didn't even own a skirt.

"Kaitlin, hurry up—you're going to miss the bus," Mom yelled up the stairs. "Tom is waiting to leave."

"Couldn't you drive us the first day?" I yelled back.

"I'm not driving you," she called back. "Meeting kids at the bus stop will be a good way to make friends." Boy, was she clueless or what?

5

She was waiting by the front door to hand me my lunch bag, and she kissed me on the forehead. "Bye, darling. Have a good first day," she said.

"Oh, sure. If my appendix doesn't burst before I get to school."

"Take care of her, Tom. I'm counting on you."

"Sure, Mom," Tom said, but when we were halfway down the front path he added under his breath, "Count on me to get her lost."

As soon as we were far enough away not to be heard, Tom turned to me and glared. "Let's get one thing straight, kid," he said. "I don't want you hanging around me at school. I don't even want you speaking to me unless it's a real emergency, got it?"

"Why not?"

He looked surprised. "Because you're a sixth grader, of course. Eighth graders don't talk to sixth graders. It's bad for the image."

Then he started to walk down the street a pace ahead of me, even though I was walking my fastest.

"Don't worry, I wouldn't even want to talk to you," I yelled after him. "I'll have my own friends to hang out with. Who needs you?"

All the way down the block I hurled angry thoughts at his back. I just hoped he knew exactly where the bus stopped. There were so many things to learn about going to a new school in a new place.

We had moved to the small town of Sonoma from San Francisco a month earlier. Our house was on a sleepy side street with lots of old fruit trees and old-fashioned flower gardens. The houses had wide front porches with rocking chairs on them. Blue jays squawked as they hopped on white fences. I liked everything about it so far, but then, I hadn't tried school yet.

I looked back down the street now, half hoping my mother had changed her mind and was getting the car out of the garage.

It was hot already. My school bag seemed to weigh a ton. I could feel hair sticking to my face. I was sure I looked like a freak in that dumb plaid skirt. At the end of the block I could see a bunch of kids hanging around on the street corner. Surely they weren't middle school kids, were they? Could those tall boys with the muscles and the baggy jeans be only eighth graders? They looked about twenty. One of them looked as if he might be starting a mustache. And those girls with the sexy ribbed crew tops and all that makeup and hair! They were staring at us with cold, unfriendly faces.

"Hey, there's Aaron," Tom said. He hurried ahead, completely forgetting about me. "Yo, Aaron, dude!"

The difference between being fourteen and being eleven is that Tom was allowed to go to the community pool alone. Having very old-fashioned and overprotective parents, I had to wait for someone to take me. So he'd already made some friends and I hadn't.

"Hey, dude, how's it going?" Aaron yelled in a big, deep voice.

"I thought you said you were riding your bike, dude," another boy said as they crowded into a tight little group, leaving me standing there alone on the sidewalk.

"I was, but my mother made me take the bus because I have to keep an eye on the kid," Tom said.

Four pairs of scary eyes were looking at me as if I were a creature from Mars.

"Hi," I said in my coolest voice.

"Sixth grader?" one of the guys asked.

"Can't you tell?" Tom said, and they all laughed. I didn't see what was funny. I just prayed the bus would hurry up and get there. But then I decided that was a dumb thing to hope for. If the bus never showed up, Mom would have to drive us, or better still, I wouldn't have to go to school. So I prayed for a flat tire instead.

I'd been really excited when I heard we were moving away from the city to a little town and that I'd be going to a big middle school. In my old school district, sixth grade was still in elementary school. My best friends, Lindsay and Anna, had been very jealous when they heard I would be in middle school.

"You'll be going to dances with eighth graders, and we're stuck with another year of elementary school," they said.

It had sounded cool and exciting at the time. I'd pictured myself drifting down the halls with my books under my arm, going to new and exciting classes, hanging out with older kids. It seemed like the perfect chance to change my image. At my old school everyone knew me. They knew I blushed when the teacher called on me. They knew I hated speaking up in class. I was quiet, nobody Kaitlin Durham. Nobody exactly hated me, but most people didn't even know I existed.

I had my own group of friends like me, but I never got invited to do things by the popular clique.

So when we moved, it seemed like this was my big chance to change my image. I'd made this vow. I wasn't going to be shy anymore. From now on I'd be cool and friendly and outgoing. I'd be popular and run for student council, and when Lindsay and Anna met me again, they'd hardly know the new, improved Kaitlin Durham with added brighteners. It had seemed like a great idea at the time. Now I wasn't so sure.

TWO

I was still in the middle of praying for the flat tire when a big old yellow school bus came rattling and rumbling down the block. All the other kids pushed ahead of me as if I didn't exist, including my brother. By the time I got on, there were almost no seats left. Some kids had their backpacks on the seats beside them, and they didn't look as if they were about to move them. So much for the new, instantly popular, cool Kaitlin! I stood there, feeling more like a geek than ever, trying to decide if I dared ask anyone to move their things, or if I'd rather stand all the way to school. That problem was solved for me.

"We're not going anywhere until everyone takes a seat," the bus driver roared. He was a grouchy-looking old man, and I could see him looking at me in the rearview mirror. "Little lady, find yourself a bench and park your carcass."

Some kids giggled. I moved hopefully toward a round-faced boy. He had only a lunch bag on the seat. It wouldn't be too much to ask him to move that, would it? But he put his hand on the bag and glared at me. "No way," he said.

I was getting hotter and hotter. I could feel all those eyes watching me. Then a light, sweet voice spoke up behind me. "You can sit here if you like."

I looked around. The voice belonged to a girl about my age, a tiny bit chubby, with shining brown hair and big, serious dark eyes behind wire-frame glasses. She had two little frown lines between her eyes. She was wearing jeans and a T-shirt that said Thumbelina Horse Ranch. Gratefully I sank into the seat beside her, and the bus roared away.

"Thanks," I said. "I thought the bus driver was going to throw me off the bus. It's no fun when you don't know anybody. My name's Kaitlin."

"I'm Emily," she said. "You don't know anybody, either?"

I shook my head. "We just moved here from San Francisco. How about you?"

"I live way out of town on a ranch. My elementary school only had fifty kids in five grades."

"Wow, only ten kids per grade!"

She grinned. "Math whiz, huh?"

When she smiled, she looked quite different. Her whole face just lit up. I'd read about twinkling eyes before, but I'd never actually seen them. Emily's eyes really twinkled. When I'd first noticed her, she had this bored, superior look. But that may just have been the glasses, or perhaps she didn't want people to know that she was scared.

"Nice outfit," she said.

"Are you serious?"

"Yes, I really like it. I get so bored with jeans

and jeans and more jeans. But my mother would say something like that wasn't practical for where we live."

I was looking at her T-shirt. "You said you live on a ranch? Thumbelina Horse Ranch—is that it?"

She nodded.

"You're so lucky," I said. "I've always wanted to take horseback riding, but my mother made me take ballet instead. Maybe I could come over and you could teach me to ride your horses sometime."

Emily started to laugh. "I'd like to see you ride our horses," she said. "They're only two feet high."

"That's impossible."

"It's true. My mother breeds miniature horses."

Oh, I get it, I thought. I'll bet she thinks I don't know anything because I'm from the city. She's just making that up about the miniature horses. I wasn't going to give her a chance to laugh at me, so I decided to change the subject.

"Do you have any brothers or sisters?"

"A little brother," she said, "and I have a new step-sister who's about the same age as me."

"How exciting."

Emily looked at me as if she wasn't sure whether I was kidding or not. "You really think so?"

"Sure," I said. "When you're the baby, like me, everybody bosses you around and teases you. I think it would be nice to have a sister the same age as me— like getting an instant friend."

Emily made a face. "I don't even know her. I've seen her a couple of times, but she lives with her

12

mother. I didn't like her much at the wedding. She was a real snob."

"Is your stepdad nice?"

"He's okay," Emily said, and she looked out the window again. "He wants to act like my father, but I've already got a real father, so why do I need another one?"

I couldn't answer that, because I still had both my parents. There were times when I would have willingly traded both of them, but I was glad our family had never had to go through a divorce, like some of my friends' families.

"So you're the baby in your family?" she asked.

I nodded. "I have a sister in high school, and that's my brother showing off for those girls up there. The one with the short blond hair and the Forty-Niners shirt."

"He didn't even let you sit with him on the bus!" Emily exclaimed. "What a jerk."

"Total jerk," I said. "Now that he's an eighth grader, he acts like he's Mr. Macho all the time."

"Are you going into sixth grade?" Emily asked.

I nodded.

"Me, too. What homeroom do you have?"

"Mrs. Bliese."

"Me, too!"

We grinned delightedly at each other. I felt much better now. I knew somebody. I had someone to help me find Mrs. Bliese's room.

"Now I have someone who can help me find my way around," Emily said.

"That's just what I was thinking!" I exclaimed, and we laughed. I was already liking Emily.

The school bus passed the Sonoma town square, with its park in the middle, surrounded by old historic buildings, and finally swung in through the gates of a new-looking steel-and-glass building. It looked to me as if all four hundred students were arriving at the same time, and what's more, they all seemed to know where they were going. Almost all of them were wearing jeans or shorts or overalls like the ones I'd wanted. There were no plaid kilts to be seen. I'd tell my mom that when I got home. If I didn't make friends, it would be all her fault for making me look so geeky.

I stayed close to Emily as we got off the bus. Tom looked back once in my direction.

"Great," he said. "You've made a friend. See ya," and he sprinted to catch up with the other eighth-grade guys. So much for brotherly love. So much for obeying Mom's orders. It occurred to me that I could get him in big trouble if I wanted to. I grinned to myself as I imagined telling Mom a terrible tale about getting lost and not finding my classroom all morning because Tom left me alone at the bus. That would teach him not to act like a big shot.

Luckily for Tom, there were big signs up pointing to all the classrooms and even a couple of teachers directing sixth graders, so there was no possibility we'd get lost.

Emily and I found our way easily to room 107. Our teacher, Mrs. Bliese, was big and motherly looking. "Find an empty seat wherever you like," she said. "I'll be taking attendance in a few minutes and assigning you your locker numbers."

"I'm glad she didn't make us sit in alphabetical order," I said. "We might have been on opposite sides of the classroom."

"Why, what's your name?"

"Durham," I said.

Emily started laughing. "Mine's Delgado," she said. "I'll bet we would have been next to each other anyway."

We stood there, looking around the classroom for empty seats together. It seemed we were the only newcomers. Everybody else was talking, leaning across aisles, or turning around in their seats. Two boys were playing ticktacktoe, passing a paper back and forth. A couple of girls at the back were brushing their hair. Mrs. Bliese didn't seem to mind.

Nobody paid any attention to me. I was glad in a way. I didn't want to go through another bus-stop ordeal, with everyone staring at me as if a cockroach had just come into the classroom. But a friendly "Hi, you're new here, right?" might have been nice.

As we walked to our seats a huge guy in overalls called out to Emily, "Yo, Delgado, what are you doing here?"

"Taking flying lessons, Pee Wee, what do you think," Emily said, and rolled her eyes.

"Ugh, Pee Wee Pugh," she muttered when she was safely past him. "Of all the people in the world I have to get in my homeroom, it had to be him. He is so disgusting."

"Is that his name? Pee Wee Pugh?" I said, starting to giggle.

"No, his real name is Billy, but he's always been called Pee Wee, on account of his being so big," she said.

That didn't sound right to me. Clearly there were different rules out of the city.

We found two seats behind each other, near the back of the classroom. Mrs. Bliese started calling roll.

"Adams, Sam?"

"Here."

"Atkinson, Stephanie?"

"Present."

I looked around as each kid answered, trying to memorize names and faces. I'd never had to handle a situation like this before. I'd gone from preschool to kindergarten with a lot of the same kids. We'd moved from grade to grade together. I'd never in my life been in a room with thirty strangers. Make that twenty-nine. I already knew Emily.

"Crawley, Cindy."

"Present."

I was trying to count how many names came before mine, so I'd be ready to answer and I wouldn't come out with some strange sound.

"Delgado, Emily?"

"Here," Emily said in a high little squeak. Boy, she was more nervous than I was.

"Durham, Kaitlin."

I opened my mouth to say "Here," and it came out more like a frog croak. Heads turned to see who had made the weird noise. Strike that about Emily being more nervous than me. Nobody could be more nervous than me!

I could feel the glow coming from my face as I looked down and pretended to be busy taking stuff from my backpack and arranging pencils on my desk. I glanced to one side of me, and a guy with bright red hair and a lot of freckles gave me a grin. It was good to know there was someone in the class with more freckles than me. I wasn't sure whether he was trying to be friendly or he was grinning because of the weird sound I'd made or because I was blushing. I sort of gave him a half grin back as Mrs. Bliese called, "Sanders, Ryan?"

"Here." So the red-haired guy was Ryan Sanders. At least I knew one name.

Roll call was almost over when the door burst open, and a girl came in. She stood in the doorway for a second, looking around the room. "Am I supposed to be here?" she asked dramatically.

Mrs. Bliese was at a loss for words for a second. She just stared at the new girl. So did everyone else. I could understand why, because I was staring, too. She certainly looked different. Everyone else in the room was definitely low-key—you know, faded jeans, T-shirts, overalls. This girl was wearing a very bright purple, yellow, and red tunic over black leggings, and a woven headband around her forehead. The headband didn't manage to tame the biggest mane of black spiral curls in the universe. I'd never seen so much hair. I had a Cut and Style Barbie at home, and even she didn't have that much hair!

Mrs. Bliese managed to compose herself. "What's your name, dear?"

"Alexis Alexandra Taylor," the girl said. "But you can call me Lexie. Most people do."

"Very well . . . uh . . . Lexie," Mrs. Bliese said. She was clearly rattled by now. She picked up the class list and studied it. "Yes, you're definitely supposed to be here."

"Great," Lexie said. "Sorry I'm late. I was following this interesting black leather jacket with a bald eagle on the back, and I wound up in seventh grade by mistake. It took a while for the teacher to realize that I wasn't supposed to be there."

I could imagine that Lexie had that effect on people. Some of the kids giggled, and some of them, who obviously knew her from previous encounters, called out things like, "Nice try, Lexie." Or, "Only you could think up an excuse like that." Or, "You trying to cut sixth grade totally, Lexie?"

Lexie acted as though she hadn't even heard them and didn't even notice their existence. She was looking around grandly, exactly like a queen standing in front of her subjects. I had never seen anyone so cool in my life. Why couldn't I be like that? She turned back to Mrs. Bliese. "I mean, I'd never have followed the jacket in the first place, only the bald eagle was painted incorrectly. Bald eagles have yellow eyes, not black. Everyone who's into conservation knows that, don't they?"

Mrs. Bliese tried to regain control. "Why don't you find yourself a seat, Lexie. Let's see where there's a spare one."

"I have a friend saving me a seat, thank you," Lexie said, and swept down the aisle, her tunic billowing against people sitting on either side. Heads turned to see where she would end up. To my amazement, she stopped beside me and gave me her most brilliant smile. "Hey, how's it going?" she said, and plopped into the chair beside me.

THREE

Lexie didn't have a chance to say much more to me because Mrs. Bliese was handing out locker assignments and then class schedules. I acted like I was paying attention to Mrs. Bliese, but really I was thinking about Lexie. Had she mistaken me for someone else? What if she called me by someone else's name when we finally had a chance to talk and then said, "Sorry, I got you mixed up with another girl I used to know"?

That would be embarrassing, and in a way I'd be sorry, because it would mean that Lexie wouldn't be my friend after all. I got my class schedule, and I turned around to compare with Emily. We both had math second period, only it turned out that she had prealgebra and I had math 6. She had gifted social studies, too.

"Let's see." Lexie leaned across to compare with us. "Oh, we have the same GATE class," she said to Emily. "Cool!"

"What's GATE?" I asked. I had art exploration that period.

"It stands for 'gifted and talented,'" Lexie said smoothly.

20

"Oh." I couldn't think of anything else to say. It seemed I was the only dummy around. I'd never thought of myself as dumb before, but now that I was getting art exploration while everyone around me was going somewhere else to be gifted and talented, I wasn't so sure. I wasn't sure of anything. This first day was definitely not turning out as I had hoped: twenty-nine students who weren't talking to me, one who was in all gifted classes, and one who was both cool and unique and said she was my friend when she didn't even know me! No wonder I felt confused, and all I wanted right now was to be back in my old elementary school. I was already praying for next June.

The bell rang, and Emily went off to be gifted, and Lexie went somewhere else, and I stuck around for math. I managed fine through English, and then I saw that I had PE fourth period. Somehow I had to find my way to the gym. I'd been shown the gym when I came to orientation. It was very big, and it stuck out at the back of the school—which should mean it was easy enough to find, right? A big noisy group of kids was leaving the classroom ahead of me, so I tagged along behind them. It seemed like the simplest way to get to the gym without having to ask for directions and look like a megadweeb.

Down the front hall to the end, then we turned left. So far, so good. Then we left the main hall and turned into a side hallway. Someone opened a door, and we stepped into the art room. I tried to back away without being seen as the kids I'd been following sat down at the easels. I stood there in the hallway, trying to stay calm. Okay, no need for panic yet. I was in a school building, not a maze. The gym couldn't be too far away. If I kept walking long enough, I'd have to come to it, right? So I kept on down the hall and around a corner and found myself in a part of the school I'd never seen before in my life.

The halls were emptying as class started. Maybe they'd moved the gym since I had orientation. Maybe it was now tucked away in some far-off corner of the campus, on the other side of the football field. Maybe I'd been zapped into a parallel universe—I was ready to believe anything.

Doors were closing. I could hear the sound of teachers' voices droning. I was so mad at myself. How could I be the only student in the entire school who was lost? No wonder I wasn't in the gifted program. I wasn't even sure which way to walk anymore. I was beginning to imagine that they'd come across my whitened bones at the end of the school year.

Then I saw rescue coming in the shape of Emily.

"Emily," I yelled.

She turned to my voice and gave me that big, twinkling smile. "Kaitlin, I'm so glad to see you. Where's the gym?"

"I'm looking for it, too," I said. "I wound up in art by mistake."

"I was following this map I made," Emily said, "but I must have gotten it upside down."

She held out the map to me, and we examined it. I never was too good at reading maps, and I couldn't tell a thing from this one.

"I just knew I'd get lost, so I went to the trouble of making a map, but now I think I might have put something down wrong," she said.

I felt so much better already. At least she wasn't totally gifted and talented in everything. It was reassuring to know that she made mistakes like normal people.

We were both poring over the map when we heard someone yelling down the hall. "Don't tell me you guys are lost?"

It was Lexie, hair and tunic flying out behind her as she ran to join us.

There was no way I was going to let someone as confident as Lexie know that I was hopelessly lost.

"Us lost? Nah. We were just hanging out between classes," I started to say, but Emily's voice cut right over mine. "We're trying to find the gym, Lexie. Can you show us the way?"

Lexie didn't laugh or tell us we were hopeless. Instead she took the map and examined it. "The gym, huh? That's where I'm heading," she said. "Just follow me. I know a shortcut, so we're not late."

She started off down the hall, with Emily and me running to keep up with her. At the end she swung to the right and paused outside a door. "If my calculations are correct," she said, tossing back that impressive hair, "this door leads to the locker rooms."

We wrenched open the door, walked by a huge closet, and found ourselves in the middle of a biology lab. What's more, it was full of students—older kids, like the ones at the bus stop. They all looked up as we burst into their classroom.

The teacher was a tall, skinny guy, and he was in the middle of talking, while he held up something in a glass jar. "Would anyone like to hazard a guess as to what kind of creature this is that we will be dissecting first?" he asked.

"Looks like a sixth grader to me!" yelled a voice. It was my brother, Tom, and he was grinning like an idiot as the rest of the class burst out laughing.

My cheeks were burning with embarrassment as we fled from the room. How could he do this to me? What kind of brother was that?

"Thanks a lot, Lexie," I snapped. "Why did you pretend you knew the way to the gym when you're just as lost as we are? You made us look like total fools."

"Well, sorreee," she said, looking at me defiantly. "I thought I'd made a lucky guess. So I was wrong."

"And another thing," I demanded, now that I was good and mad and on a roll. "Why did you tell Mrs. Bliese that I was your friend?"

She didn't even blink as she stared back at me. "Because I thought you looked nice," she said.

"Oh." For the second time that morning I was speechless. I was beginning to think that Lexie always had that effect on people.

"We'd better find the gym quickly or we'll be in real trouble," Emily said, grabbing my arm. She started to half drag me down the hall, until at last we came to an alcove. Inside it were two doors. They said Girls' Locker Room and Boys' Locker Room.

"We've made it," Lexie said. "I knew we would if we kept on down this way."

I wanted to tell her that she'd made us go the other way, but I shut up. After all, she had picked me from the whole class because she thought I looked nice. So I followed her into the locker room. The last girls were just tying their shoes, ready to run out into the gym. We struggled into our PE shorts and shirts as fast as we could, but by the time we got to the gym, the whole class was sitting on the floor and the teacher was already talking.

"Boy, are we going to be in trouble," Emily muttered.

But Lexie shook her head. "I'd say we've lucked out," she whispered. "Take a look at the teacher. What a hunk. He looks like he should be lifeguarding on Malibu Beach."

She was right. The teacher certainly was a hunk. Young—for a teacher—with big muscles, a great tan, sun-streaked blond hair, and bright blue eyes. Wow!

He must have noticed us staring at him, because he looked in our direction as we stood in the doorway.

"Are you girls supposed to be part of this class?" he asked. He even had a deep, sexy voice.

"Yes, sir," Emily said. "We're sorry we're late, but we couldn't find our way to the gym."

A slow smile spread over the teacher's face, but it wasn't exactly the friendly, welcoming smile we'd expected.

"What do you think, that I look so young that I'm only just out of teachers college or something?"

I looked at Emily. Emily looked at me. Neither of us could understand what he was getting at. But we didn't have to, because he went on. "I've been around long enough to know what goes on in girls' locker rooms. You sit there gossiping, and you fix your hair, and you fix everyone else's hair, and when you finally notice the time . . . guess what, you're ten minutes late for class."

"That's so sexist," Lexie muttered.

"That wasn't—" I began, but he held up his hand.

"No excuses, please. I know all the creative excuses that middle school students can think up, so don't insult me by expecting me to believe that the dog ate your gym suits."

Some kids giggled. I was feeling hot and embarrassed again, because I hated teachers to get the wrong idea about me and I hated taking the blame for something that wasn't really my fault. But I didn't think that this was a good time to argue with him, even if I did have the nerve to speak up.

"Okay, come on and join the others," he said. "I was just telling everyone else that they should understand right now that PE is not going to be a Mickey Mouse class. It is not an easy A. I don't give out A's just for showing up and breathing. I expect everyone in full PE uniform—every day. No excuses. And I expect everyone to be on time in the future. Anyone who shows up after I call roll will have to do fifty sit-ups. Is that clear?"

There was a sort of group mumble from the kids on the floor.

"Okay. For the benefit of those students who have just arrived, my name is Mr. Meany."

"Meany by name. Meany by nature," Lexie said, loud enough for the kids in front of us to hear. They

26

turned around and grinned. I just prayed Mr. Meany hadn't heard.

". . . and I want you all to wear name tags until I've learned your names. Everyone get up and write yourself a name tag now. There are markers and name tags on the table. When you're done, start running in place for our warm-up."

We went over to the table. Lexie took a pen and wrote Amanda Schlottkiss in big letters.

"Lexie!" Emily said in horror.

Lexie grinned. "He was rude to us. He didn't believe us. As far as I'm concerned, he doesn't deserve to know our right names. You can call yourself Consuela, and Kaitlin can call herself Frederika—Frederika Frumpen-haus."

"We'd get in trouble," Emily said, but she had to laugh. I was laughing, too. Really, Lexie was too outrageous, but I had to admit that she was fun. I just imagined running around with a name tag that said Frederika Frumpenhaus on me, but I didn't dare write it. Neither did Emily. I saw her printing Emily Delgado in neat letters. Lexie put the Amanda Schlottkiss name on her T-shirt and started running in place.

After the running came jumping jacks. One hundred of them.

"Our first PE unit is called physical conditioning," Mr. Meany said as we jumped up and down, panting hard. "We'll start out with a lot of aerobics, including jogging, and strength and flexibility exercises. My aim is that every student will leave this class in superb physical shape," Mr. Meany called as we clapped our hands over our heads.

"Or dead," Lexie muttered.

There were giggles around us. Mr. Meany gave a cold stare in our direction. Clearly he was already thinking of us as troublemakers. I'd always been a good student at my old school. My parents were very hot on politeness and good behavior, and I knew how they'd overreact if I got in any kind of trouble. So I tried extra hard, moving my arms with the grace of all that ballet training, hoping Mr. Meany would notice.

After the jumping jacks he started to test us for fitness on sit-ups, push-ups, chin-ups—all that kind of stuff. Mr. Meany said that he was going to test us again at the end of the year and we'd be surprised at how much we'd improved.

It was pretty obvious right away that my friends and I were not exactly the world's greatest jocks. I could do two chin-ups, but Emily couldn't even manage one. Of course, she does have more weight to carry around, and I'll bet that gifted and talented brain weighs a lot.

Then it was Lexie's turn. Mr. Meany called out her name from his roster, and she stepped over to the chin-up bar.

"I called Alexis Taylor," Mr. Meany said.

"That's me," Lexie answered.

"But your name tag says Amanda Schlottkiss," Mr. Meany said.

Lots of giggles this time.

"Oh, wow, how dumb of me," Lexie said. "I must have picked up someone else's name tag by mistake. I'll go and write another one."

"You'll stay and do chin-ups," Mr. Meany said, giving her that hard stare again. She managed two, like me.

"Don't worry, Alexis," Mr. Meany said as she returned to her place. "By the end of the year we'll have you whipped into shape."

I knew he was talking about more than the physical exercises. It was going to be war between Lexie and Mr. Meany!

FOUR

By the time the bell rang for lunch, I found that I was starving, which surprised me. The way my stomach had felt that morning, I didn't think I'd ever be able to eat again. I expected to be in the recovery room minus my appendix by lunchtime. But here I was, clutching my lunch bag, heading toward the outdoor tables with Lexie on one side of me and Emily on the other.

We hadn't said much as we changed after PE, but it was like we'd made an arrangement that we were going to eat together, because Emily and Lexie waited for me while I tried to get my flyaway hair to stay down. It was cool and shady outside under big maples and pines, but the tables were filled with what looked like all four hundred kids. Every time we tried to sit, someone growled, "This table's taken."

Eventually we gave up and went to sit on the steps of the outdoor amphitheater, which was in the sun and therefore hot, but less crowded.

"What a morning. My nerves are definitely frazzled," Emily said. "I just hope a chocolate-chip brownie will soothe me."

"Chocolate-chip brownies?" I said. My mouth was watering.

"Yes, my grandmother bakes them. They're really good and gooey. You want to try some?"

"I'd love to, if you have enough," I said.

"Here." Emily took out a huge brownie and broke it into three pieces.

"You don't know how good this looks." I sighed. "My mother's into healthy stuff. She reads tons of books on nutrition and studies the labels for fat content. I'll bet I can guess what's in my lunch. It has to be turkey breast." I opened the bag and pulled out the sandwich. "I was right—turkey breast and sprouts on whole wheat, apple juice to drink, a large apple for a snack, and a bag of oat-bran raisin cookies, baked by my mother."

"Sounds okay to me," Emily said.

"Okay, but boring."

"Then tell her you want something different," Lexie said, sounding surprised.

"You don't know my mother," I said. "She's the type who thinks she knows best—always."

"Parents are a pain," Emily said.

"Not if you use psychology," Lexie said. "I can always get around my mother if I say what she wants to hear."

"Like what?"

"Okay, you tell her you want to save her from the extra chore of making your lunch, now that you're a mature and responsible middle school student," Lexie suggested. "Then you can put what you want in it."

31

"That's not a bad idea," I said. I was thinking that I could buy junk snacks at the cafeteria with my allowance.

"Parents always fall for the mature-and-responsible line. Try it on her. I'll bet it works," Lexie said, giving me that dazzling smile.

"Thanks, I will." It sounded simple. After all, if Tom was old enough to make his own lunch, so was I.

"I am an expert," Lexie said. "There is nothing I can't get my parents to do, especially if I play one against the other, which is what our family therapist said I do. If I say Dad thinks something is a good idea, I know my mother is going to hate it, and the other way, too. It's so simple."

Emily looked at me with a questioning smile. Obviously she hadn't met anyone like Lexie before, either.

Lexie gave a big, dramatic sigh. "I wish it was as easy to solve the Mr. Meany problem. He has to go." She took a Tupperware bowl filled with cold pasta out of her bag and started eating. "It's either him or me."

"I think you'd better learn to get along with him, Lexie," Emily said seriously. "If anyone went, it would be you. Probably straight into detention, without passing Go."

"Then I'm just going to have to whip him into shape," Lexie said with a wicked grin. "You guys can help me come up with ideas. I had great success with a teacher named Mrs. Hodgkins at my school in L.A. She had to start seeing a shrink after she had me."

"You were at school in Los Angeles?" I asked, surprised. "Then how come the other kids know you here?"

"We live here when my mother's not working," Lexie said.

"What kind of work does she do?" Emily asked.

"She's a movie star," Lexie said carelessly, "so we go down south whenever she has to shoot a movie."

"Your mother's a movie star? What's her name?" Emily asked excitedly.

"Her professional name is Lana Daniels," Lexie said.

"I've never heard of her. What movies has she been in?" I asked.

"Oh, hundreds of movies. She's been on TV, in commercials . . . You'd know her if you saw her. She's very beautiful. She has long blond hair—"

"Blond?" I couldn't help blurting, because Lexie didn't look as if she could possibly have a blond mother.

Lexie looked at me with that unblinking stare of hers. "My mom's white and my dad's black," she said. "My dad is a famous TV news cameraman. He lives in Mill Valley when he's not traveling around the world. I get to spend weekends with him."

"Are they divorced?" I asked.

"Of course," Lexie said. "Otherwise he'd live with us, wouldn't he?"

I was beginning to wonder if this wasn't another made-up story, like the one about Emily's miniature horses. After all, Lexie had written the wrong name on her tag. Maybe she was great at inventing things. Maybe she'd just made up a movie star mother and a

33

TV news father, and her parents were really ordinary people—store clerks or insurance agents or even bankers like my dad.

She must have sensed I was staring at her because she stared right back, not even blinking. This made me uncomfortable, so I turned to Emily. "That was a great brownie. You're so lucky to have a grandmother who bakes."

"She's a great cook," Emily said. "You should taste her burritos and enchiladas." She said the words with the right sort of accent.

"Does your family come from Mexico?" Lexie asked her.

"They did a long time ago," Emily said. "My dad's grandfather came here and started a vineyard before World War Two. But they still keep up a lot of the traditions, like great Mexican cooking."

"Do you speak Spanish?" I asked.

Emily laughed. "I can say *buenos días*, and that's about it. But I'm going to take Spanish next year. We still have relatives in Mexico I've never met. It would be cool to visit them and be able to talk to them."

Lexie leaned back and let her hair trail onto the concrete step behind her. "So what about you?" she asked me. "Did you just move here?"

I nodded. "We moved out from the city."

"I just adore San Francisco," Lexie said with a sigh. "It's so romantic and exciting. Why would you want to move out here where it's so boring?"

"It was my parents' idea, not mine," I said. "They

34

started freaking about the crime. They'd never let us go out anywhere alone. So they decided to move here, where it's safe and we could ride our bikes and have the kind of life they had as kids."

"Does your father live with you?"

"Of course."

"And your mom doesn't work?"

"Only at home," I said. "She's got lots of volunteer activities."

"Are your parents for real?" Lexie asked.

"Yes. Why?"

Lexie grinned. "Mom and Dad still live together, and Mom bakes oatmeal cookies and makes her kids lunches and volunteers. They sound like something out of an old TV show."

I could feel myself blushing. "Sorry. I can't help my parents. It's the way they are."

"I think they sound perfect," Emily said. "Kaitlin's lucky."

"It doesn't always feel that way," I said. "My mother has too much time to fuss over us."

"And what does your dad do?" Lexie went on.

There was no way I could make working in a bank sound interesting, not after Emily's horses and Lexie's movie star mother and both of them being gifted and talented. "He likes everyone to think that he works in a bank," I said, dropping my voice, "but actually he's employed by the CIA."

"No kidding?" Emily said. "You mean he's a spy?"

"Keep your voice down," I said, looking around. "He'd kill me if he knew I was talking about it. I'm

35

not really supposed to know what he does, but I was snooping around in his study once, looking for the Liquid Paper, and I found all these instructions in code in his desk. After that I kept tabs on him, and when he went away."

"Oh, wow," Emily said. Even Lexie looked impressed. I was amazed at myself for coming up with this. I had no idea I was so creative. I couldn't believe this was me talking. I felt kind of guilty, because I wasn't usually the kind of person who told lies, but this lie was different. It went along with baby horses and movie stars.

"That's why we moved out here," I went on. "We had to get out of the city in a hurry. My dad wanted us to live somewhere safe—you know, because of terrorists. But don't ever mention any of this if you meet him. He doesn't think I know anything about it."

"We won't," Emily said. "How exciting. You could write a book one day."

"We must meet him soon," Lexie said. "I'm dying to know what a real spy looks like."

"Ordinary," I said. "That's why nobody ever suspects."

"I saw a movie like that once," Lexie said. "The spy was the most mild-mannered man. That's so neat. When can we meet him?"

I hadn't considered this possibility—Lexie asking him questions, dropping hints that she "knew." I felt hot and cold as I thought of it. "You have to promise that you'll act normal around him."

"Oh, sure," Lexie said. "I met George Lucas once. I can be cool."

"Where do you live, Kaitlin?" Emily asked.

"On Elm Street."

"Nightmare on Elm Street! I love it," Lexie yelled.

"It is kind of nightmarish. That big old Victorian house with the turret."

"Are you serious?" Emily said, her face lighting up. "I love that house. I've always wanted to see inside it. Who gets the turret room?"

"My brother," I said.

"How come not you?" Lexie asked. "I'd have fought him for it."

"We did fight for it. He won," I said. I didn't add that I hadn't fought very hard. I was kind of scared of being alone on the attic floor, a whole staircase away from the rest of the family.

"Too bad," Lexie said. "It would have been great to have a sleepover up in the turret room . . . especially on a stormy night. Real spooky."

"Yeah!" Emily said.

I looked from one face to the other. I'd met them only a few hours ago, and already they were talking about sleepovers. And I'd been scared that I wouldn't make any friends here.

"I just love sleepovers, don't you?" Lexie said, sitting up again and hugging her knees.

"I love them, too," Emily said, "although I haven't been to many. The kids at my old school weren't into sleepovers very much. They had to get up for farm chores, and they weren't fun like you and Kaitlin."

"Do you like sleepovers, KD?" Lexie asked.

"What did you call her?" Emily said.

"KD. It's my name for her," Lexie said. "You have to admit that Kaitlin Durham sounds like a boring lady newscaster, so I'm going to use her initials from now on."

"KD," Emily said. "I like it. It suits her."

I liked it, too. Nobody had ever given me a nickname before.

"I love sleepovers," I said. "They're one of my favorite things."

Lexie picked up her bowl and started waving the fork around. "Sleepovers on weekends and no Mr. Meany—these are a few of my favorite things," she sang in a great Julie Andrews imitation.

I didn't want to say that even though I loved sleepovers, my mother didn't. In fact, I had to beg, plead, and squirm to ever get her to allow me to sleep over anywhere, even at Lindsay's or Anna's house. She always said I was cranky in the mornings and got sick after sleepovers—which wasn't true. I'm cranky every morning if I'm woken up too early.

"We must plan a sleepover," Lexie said. "Hey, you know what? This school year is going to be fun after all. I thought it was going to be a real downer after getting back from L.A., but now I'm looking forward to it."

"Me, too," Emily said. Her face was all bright and sparkling again. "You don't know how great it is to be at a real school with real people after five years of Pee Wee Pugh and his gross friends making animal noises and pulling my braids."

38

An hour earlier I had been sitting thinking how much I missed my old friends and my old school and how I'd never fit in here. But now I realized that there was a lot to look forward to. Whatever happened this year, with Emily and Lexie around it wouldn't be boring.

"It's going to be totally fun," I said.

FIVE

By the end of Tuesday, I'd gotten my new school down pat. I could find my way around without tying a string from my locker. I had actually talked to other kids in my class, and I knew some names. Ryan Sanders grinned when I looked in his direction and said hi when he passed me on the way to his desk. I got the feeling that maybe he liked me. Maybe he thought that freckle-faced people should stick together.

I liked most of my teachers, and art exploration was definitely going to be fun. I was kind of glad that I wasn't gifted and talented, because the students were going to be writing their own play in that period and I was getting to play with clay and make masks and all kinds of neat stuff.

And I had two new friends.

One of my old friends, Anna, called me on Wednesday evening to see how things were going. It was great to hear from her, but it was a surprise, too. So much had happened since we moved that Anna seemed like someone from a whole lifetime ago.

"It isn't the same without you, Kaitlin. We really miss you so much," she said.

"I miss you guys, too," I said. I did miss them, but not as much as I thought I would. In fact, I hadn't thought about them since Monday.

"So what's it like being a cool middle school student?" she asked.

"Cool." I told her about everything that had happened, trying not to make it sound as if I was acting superior. She was very envious of our eating lunch outside and having different teachers for all our classes. "You're so lucky." She sighed. "You'll never guess who we're stuck with. Miss Catchpole."

"That old, old teacher?"

"You got it. She's been teaching sixth grade for at least fifty years. Talk about boring."

Then she said, kind of casually, "So, have you made any new friends yet?" I told her about Emily and Lexie. When I described Lexie, she laughed, and I could tell she thought Lexie was weird. I didn't mention the movie star part because I wasn't sure about it.

"I can't imagine you being in trouble in gym class," Anna said. "That just isn't like you. You used to die of embarrassment if the teacher even looked at you."

"I'm learning to handle it," I said.

"How's your bratty brother doing? Is he acting like Mr. Cool eighth grader?"

"Not anymore," I said, glancing over my shoulder at the living room, where my parents were watching

TV. "The girls on the bus think he's a pain, and he's in big trouble already."

"No kidding. What did he do?"

"He got a really low score on his math placement test yesterday and he's been put in intro to math."

"Intro to math—what's that?"

"It's like math for idiots," I said. "You get to do things like build pyramids with sugar cubes. My folks flipped out when he told them. They called the school, and they're letting him retake the test next Monday."

"I'll bet he flunked the math test on purpose so he could goof off all year," Anna said.

"I know he did," I said, "and you want to know what else?" I peeked back into the living room again in case Tom was listening. I didn't want an already mad brother on my case. "He's got detention tomorrow."

"Detention, the first week? What did he do?"

I lowered my voice. "He got into a food fight in the cafeteria."

"I'll bet your parents freaked out."

"No kidding. You'd have thought he robbed a store or mugged an old lady. Mom and Dad gave him this long lecture and made it sound like he was one step away from San Quentin. And he's been grounded this weekend."

"Oh, well, they can't expect to have three little angels in one family, can they?" Anna said. "You and Christine have always been perfect children."

It crossed my mind that my parents might not think I was such a little angel if they knew about Mr. Meany. After I'd said good-bye to Anna and promised to visit her soon, I went into the living room to pick up my book bag.

"I have to do my homework now," I said. "Anna says hi."

Mom gave me a smile to let me know I was her good child. "You see, Tom. Kaitlin doesn't have to be reminded to do her homework," she said.

Tom glared at me as I headed up the stairs. I knew my brother was the world's biggest pain, but secretly I felt sorry for him. All he'd done was throw a few tortillas around as if they were Frisbees. No big deal. I began to wonder what my folks would say if they ever found out about my behavior in gym class. My mother would totally lose it if a teacher called to say I was acting up, especially right after Tom had disgraced the family name. But it wasn't easy to stay on Mr. Meany's good side, especially with Lexie beside me.

In the few days that we had been in his class, I think his hair was beginning to turn from sun-streaked blond to worry-streaked gray. And I could tell he still hadn't made up his mind about us, or rather about Lexie. You could almost see him thinking as he watched her, Was she really a problem child or just incredibly stupid?

We were almost late every morning, once because Lexie could only find one tennis shoe and didn't want to hop through aerobics, and once because Emily's zipper got stuck on her shorts. We skidded into place just as Mr. Meany was finishing up the roll.

"Couldn't find your way again?" he asked.

"Lost my tennis shoe," Lexie answered.

He gave us his famous hard stare.

Only Lexie could climb the rope to the very top on our arm-strength test, but then she lost her nerve. She wouldn't come down again because she said she was afraid of heights and was feeling dizzy. So Mr. Meany had to climb up himself and bring her down. It wasn't the easiest thing in the world to climb a rope and bring down a hysterical Lexie with a whole class watching. Mr. Meany's face was bright red by the time he reached the bottom. When Lexie said, "Thank you so much. You saved my life," Mr. Meany only said, "Humph."

Emily and I weren't quite sure whether Lexie did things like that on purpose or whether things just happened to her. Because things certainly happened! I thought she was trying to improve her image and be helpful when she volunteered to get out the balls Mr. Meany wanted. But when she opened the equipment closet, about a zillion big rubber balls bounced out and a flying hail of hockey sticks cascaded down on her.

By the end of the week I was doomed, along with Emily and Lexie, whether I liked it or not. The other kids thought we were total airheads. Mr. Meany thought we were dangerous.

Then came Friday.

"For the last day of our fitness testing," Mr. Meany said, rubbing his hands together as if he was delighted with what was about to happen, "we will have the endurance test."

"We're going to have to cross Death Valley with no water," Lexie whispered.

"This test is a half-mile run around the perimeter

of the campus," Mr. Meany went on, staring hard at Lexie. "And for the benefit of those students who don't get things easily, I'll draw the route on the blackboard. We go out of the gym through this exit here and head straight for the back fence. Follow the fence around past the football field, across the front of the building, through the parking lot, and in again at the gym here. Is that clear? Any questions? Anyone feel that they might get lost?" There were giggles, and kids turned to look at us.

"Stuck-up snobs. We'll show them," Lexie muttered.

I wasn't sure how we'd show them. I knew that I wasn't the world's greatest runner. In fact, I'd been put in ballet in the first place because I had weak leg muscles and the doctor suggested it. I didn't think that Emily was the world's greatest runner, either. I had a hunch that Lexie could have been, if she put her mind to it. She was tall and skinny and probably could have been a real jock if she hadn't taken such an instant dislike to Mr. Meany.

"Half a mile," Emily said as we lined up at the gym door. "I had to run for the bus the other day, and I was totally pooped. I'll be last again, I know it."

"No, we won't," Lexie said. "Because I've got a plan."

"What? We twist our ankles going out the door? We suddenly remember we have notes from our parents saying we're allergic to grass and can't run outdoors?" Emily said.

"Good thoughts, but no," Lexie answered. "Wait until we're outside and I'll tell you."

Mr. Meany blew his whistle, and we started

running. The biggest boys and the strongest girls surged through the door first. The rest of us staggered after them.

"Okay," Lexie said. "Listen up. This is what we'll do. I know a great shortcut."

"Oh no," I said. "If it's like the last one, we'll wind up in the biology lab again."

"This one is foolproof," Lexie said. "I noticed it when Meany made the mistake of drawing the route in detail on the board. When we get to the football field, we'll duck under the bleachers, then sprint across to the bicycle sheds. Next we'll go behind the line of pine trees, past the woodshop and the portable learning lab, and then wind up on the other side of the gym. We'll just wait for the right moment to step out from the side of the woodshop and we'll look as if we've done the whole thing—except we'll have actually cut out at least half the course."

"Lexie, you're a genius," Emily gasped. She was sweating already. It was a hot day.

"What if somebody sees us?" I queried.

"That's the beauty of it," Lexie said. "If somebody sees us we just say, 'Oh, were we supposed to go to the other side of the football field? So that's where we lost everybody.' Everyone thinks we're airheads anyway."

I had to admit it did sound good, even if it did sound as if we were cheating. My own hair was beginning to stick to my forehead, and my shirt was sticking to my back. We were almost last already. I just prayed Mr. Meany wasn't watching. I wasn't at all sure we'd make it to the beginning of the football field. Pee Wee Pugh stopped running and stood there wiping his face as we ran past him.

"Go, Delgado. Woo-ee! Look at her go. Faster than a speeding bullet," he yelled.

Emily didn't have the strength to yell anything back. Her mouth was set in grim determination. The bleachers were looming ahead through a haze of sweat.

Lexie looked around. We truly were last. "Now," she said. We put on a burst of effort and ducked under the bleachers. Unless anybody looked closely, we'd be hidden from view the entire length of the football field until we came to the bicycle sheds. Nobody was looking as we sprinted across the gap behind the bleachers and made it to the coolness of the bike sheds.

From there it was a piece of cake, as my dad says. We even walked in the cool shade of the pine trees and then made a final, desperate sprint down the side of the woodshop building. Just around the corner was the gym and success. Ahead of us we could see the first runners staggering in. There were long gaps between them now, long enough for us to take our places without being noticed.

"*Now,*" Lexie whispered. We came around the corner of the woodshop building and ran straight into Mr. Meany, standing there with his arms folded and a clipboard in one hand.

"Well?" he said.

I tried to think of a brilliant excuse, but my mind was blank.

"We got lost again," Lexie said.

"Nice try," Mr. Meany said, "but not very convincing."

He took out the clipboard and started writing down everyone's times. "Jason . . . nice job. Under four minutes. Mary Beth, you're the first girl." We stood there, not knowing what to do next, while all the runners came in and Mr. Meany praised each one.

Then he turned to face Lexie. "If you think you can outsmart me, young woman, then think again. Contrary to popular belief, all PE teachers are not dumb. You're up against one of the greatest brains in Sonoma County." He looked at us and gave a superior smirk. "I'd send you around the whole course again, but you're so hopelessly unfit, you look like you're about to drop from exhaustion."

"Phew," Emily said, giving me a grateful look.

"So you can get your breath back now, and at the end of the period you can stay behind and give me one hundred sit-ups."

"One hundred?"

"Read my lips—one hundred," Mr. Meany said.

"But that's our lunch period," Lexie wailed. "We won't get to eat."

"Gee, that's too bad," Mr. Meany said. He started to head back to the gym ahead of us.

"That's child abuse, not letting kids have their lunch break," Lexie muttered.

Mr. Meany turned and looked back at her. "Did you ever think there might be such a thing as teacher abuse?" he asked.

If this was a fight, I'd say that round one had gone to Mr. Meany.

*   *   *

We were all exhausted by the time we had finished our hundred sit-ups. Mr. Meany sat on the bleachers, counting for us so that we didn't cheat. I guess he didn't trust us by now. I didn't blame him. When Emily finally hauled herself up for the hundredth time, he got to his feet. "Okay, go get showered and eat your lunch," he said, "and don't ever try to cheat on an assignment again, understand?"

"Yes, sir," we all mumbled, and staggered in the direction of the locker room.

"We'll never survive a whole year of Mr. Meany," Emily said, sinking to the bench beside her locker.

"I hate him." Lexie took off her shirt and flung it on the floor.

"We did deserve it," I said hesitantly. "We tried to get out of the assignment."

"Did you actually want to run a half mile in the heat?" Lexie demanded.

"No, but—"

"There you are. I tried to get you out of it. It would have worked, too, if Mr. Meany hadn't been such a horribly suspicious snoop."

We stood side by side in the long, tiled shower room, letting the soothing water run over us. "Something has to be done about him," Lexie said. "We'll have to think up some fiendish way of getting rid of him. We could fix the ropes so that they fall when he tries to climb them, or we could find a kid with measles to go kiss him, or we could put a rattle-snake in his gym bag—"

"Lexie!" Emily and I said at the same time.

Lexie grinned. "They were just ideas," she said. "But I guess we'd have to be more subtle than that. This needs thinking about. I'll make it my weekend assignment."

"Weekend." I sighed as we toweled off and started to dress, "Boy, does that word sound great."

"Thank goodness it's Friday," Emily agreed. "I don't think I could have held up if the week had gone on any longer."

"Yeah. TGIF! I can't wait," I said. "Two whole days to goof off, with no big homework assignments yet, like papers or anything. We should do something to celebrate surviving the first week."

"Great idea," Lexie yelled, her voice echoing around the shower room. "Let's have a sleepover tonight to celebrate."

"Yeah, let's," Emily agreed.

"It has to be at KD's house," Lexie said, "because I usually spend weekends with my dad down in Mill Valley. He only has a one-bedroom condo, and he wouldn't know how to handle three giggling girls."

"Definitely KD's house," Emily agreed. "I'm dying to see that turret room."

We finished dressing and left the locker room. I hadn't said anything about this idea yet. I was really excited about the thought of a sleepover. I really wanted to get to know Emily and Lexie better—so why was my stomach tying itself in knots again?

We came out to a sky that was rapidly clouding over. "Wow, look at that," Lexie said, dancing around excitedly. "It looks like there might be a thunderstorm later. How perfect—a night in the spooky house with a storm outside. The thunder crashing and the lightning flashing and the ghosts moaning. Have you seen any ghosts yet, KD?"

"No!" I said. I wished she hadn't brought up that subject. I'm kind of scared of things like ghosts. "Hold on a minute—I'm not sure we'll be able to sleep over at my house tonight. I haven't asked my mother yet."

"Don't you want us to come?" Emily asked, her frown lines reappearing.

"Of course I do," I said. "It's just that . . . well, my mother is kind of old-fashioned. She's British, you know. She has to approve of something before she'll give me permission."

"And you don't think she'd approve of us?" Lexie demanded.

I imagined my mother's first glimpse of Lexie's outfit. "I'm sure she would," I said carefully. "It's just that she can be difficult. It's hard to explain. It's like getting permission from the queen of England. Sometimes I feel like I'm stuck in a time warp with her."

"She has to say yes," Lexie said. "Get down on your knees and beg. Say 'pretty please with sugar on top.' That always works for me. It makes my mother laugh and she always says 'you terrible child,' and ruffles my hair and gives me what I want."

I couldn't see my mother acting like that, but then, she wasn't a movie star.

"I'll ask her as soon as I get home," I said, "and I'll call you if she says okay."

The other two were now looking at me as if I was a total dweeb.

"I don't see why it's any big thing," Lexie said. "After all, we're going to be in your room most of the time. If you think she might say no, then don't give her a chance. Wait until she's busy and then just say, 'Mom, I've got some friends coming over to spend the night, okay?'"

"Tell her we've started a Friday night sleepover club and it's your turn," Emily said. "Remind her that she wants you to fit in quickly at your new school. That should work, shouldn't it?"

"Because we really, really want to sleep over at your house and see your turret room and have the most fun time in the world," Lexie said, grabbing me and shaking my shoulders, "so make it work, okay?"

"Okay," I said, more confidently than I felt. They hadn't met my mother.

SIX

My stomach was twisting itself into knots again as I rode the bus home. I stared out the window, not really listening to what Emily was saying. I had to come up with a foolproof strategy. Somehow I had to break the news to my parents that I was intending to have a sleepover that night—without having discussed it or asked permission first. It was something I'd never done before, and now that I thought about it, I couldn't imagine my mother saying yes. And if she said no, my friends would know that I was a total baby.

I really wanted my new friends to sleep over at my house. I imagined that a sleepover with Lexie would be fun—scary, maybe, but definitely fun. But I also knew what my parents were like. When I'd been asked to sleepovers at my old school, my mother had only let me go to houses where she knew the parents. She'd given me long lectures about not staying up all night and not eating junk food because I'd get sick. Ha ha! I've never yet been to a sleepover where everyone didn't pig out on junk food. It's part of the tradition. So how could she possibly agree to a sleepover tonight, especially with girls she hadn't even met yet?

It was tough being the baby of the family, I thought. Tom and Christine were always getting to do things, like Tom being allowed to go alone to the public pool. Christine didn't even have to ask permission for most things anymore. She just said, "Mom, I'm going over to Joanie's house," and that was that. Maybe that was the way to handle my mother, I decided. If I didn't give her a chance to say no, then maybe I could surprise her into agreeing.

"Good luck," Emily said as the bus reached my stop. "See you later, I hope."

"I hope so, too. Keep your fingers crossed," I said.

Tom got off the bus ahead of me and stomped home. He was in a really bad mood. He was going to miss his first eighth-grade party.

"Too bad we won't be seeing you tonight, Durham," one of the boys yelled after him.

"Yeah, we'll enjoy your pizza for you," another yelled.

Tom looked back and made a face at them. "Thanks a lot, guys," he said. "See you Monday if I'm let out of prison by then."

He looked at me. "What are you grinning at, short stuff?"

"Nothing," I said.

Mom was in the kitchen when we got home. She was making a casserole for dinner.

"Not broccoli again," Tom complained.

"I wouldn't start if I were you," Mom said. "You're in enough trouble as it is."

Christine came in and poured herself a glass of

milk. "What a week," she said. "I'm totally exhausted. All those new people, new school, new teachers—it's just too much. Don't you know it can be really harmful to move an adolescent in the middle of high school? If I turn out all screwed up, it will be your fault."

"Yeah," Tom said. "It's also harmful in eighth grade. It's a very sensitive age."

"And it wouldn't be harmful to be beaten up by kids on your way home?" Mom said with that calm smile of hers. "That could have happened to you if we'd stayed in the city. And don't worry, Tom, because you've got plenty of time to rest up this weekend, when you're not studying. You, too, Christine. You can get an early night."

"Are you serious?" Christine exclaimed, throwing her arms up in pseudo-horror. She's gotten very dramatic recently. "I'm going to the game tonight, and then we're all going out for pizza."

"I would have been getting pizza at Aaron's house," Tom said. "*And* all of the coolest eighth graders were going to be there. But *no*. I have to stay home and study for a stupid math placement test. I'm the one person who won't be there, out of the entire eighth grade. And I'll be the only person in America studying on a Friday night."

"And whose fault is that?" Mom said. "At least you can't tell me you're having trouble making new friends. I'd say you've made too many of them already."

Tom grabbed the peanut butter and starting smearing it an inch thick onto a slice of bread. "But I

55

can still go on the bike ride tomorrow morning, right?" he demanded. "We've had it all planned for weeks. The guys will be coming out from the city."

My mother nodded seriously. "We told you that you could still do the bike ride, because you'd already made plans with your friends from the city. But that's it, Tom. The rest of the weekend you're going to be up in that room, studying your little heart out."

"Yes, Mommy," Tom growled, making my mother look at me and wink. "And how was your day, sweetie pie?" she asked. Maybe this wasn't going to be hard after all.

"Pretty good," I said. "I really like Emily and Lexie. They're so nice. You're going to like them. Especially Emily—she's so smart. Did I tell you they're both in the gifted program?"

"About a hundred times," Tom said, with his mouth full of peanut butter.

"I'm very glad you've made some nice friends already," Mom said.

"They're just dying to see the inside of our house," I said brightly. I couldn't believe how well this was going. It was like she was feeding me all the right cues. "Guess what? This was always Emily's favorite house. She said she always wanted to see inside it. Lexie thinks it looks spooky."

Mom smiled. "You must invite them over sometime."

"I just did," I said. "We all decided it would be a great idea if they came for a sleepover tonight—so that we can get to know each other better and they can see the house."

My mother had been smiling until now. I saw the smile slip from her face as I was talking. "What did you say, Kaitlin?"

"I said that my friends really wanted to come over to my house, so we thought a sleepover would be a really fun idea. You don't mind, do you? We'll be very quiet and stay up in my room, if you like."

"But, Kaitlin," Mom began, still in her calm, steady voice, even though I knew she was getting upset, "you can't just invite people over for the night without discussing it with your parents first. We don't even know these girls or their families—"

"I told you, they're both very nice," I said. I couldn't believe I had just interrupted my mother. I could feel myself getting hotter by the second. I was like a volcano, about to explode.

"I'm sure they are, honeybun," Mom said, "and of course we want you to make friends, but a sleep-over—so soon? That seems like rushing things to me. You only met them on Monday."

"You want me to make friends here, don't you?" I demanded. "You were the one who took me away from Anna and Lindsay, and now I've met two girls who actually like me, and they're both in the gifted program, and if they can't sleep over they'll probably think I don't really like them and then I'll have no-body." The words just tumbled out, faster and faster. I had meant to keep my cool, but I couldn't help it. I was very close to tears now, and I hated to cry with my brother watching.

My mother came around the kitchen table and put

her arm around my shoulders. "Don't get upset, Kaitlin. Of course we want you to make friends, and of course you can have them sleep over sometime. It's just that tonight isn't a good night, I'm afraid. Daddy and I have been invited out to dinner."

"And I'm going to the game, remember, so don't expect me to baby-sit them," Christine added as she went out of the kitchen.

"So what's the big deal, Mom?" I said, ignoring her. "Why can't we stay here alone? We're eleven years old, you know. That's officially old enough to baby-sit other people's kids. Other mothers actually trust their children with girls my age."

"They need their heads examined," Tom said.

"And Tom will be upstairs if anything happens," I added sweetly, "seeing as he's grounded and can't go to his party."

Tom stuffed the last of the peanut butter into his mouth and leaped up. "Hey, don't bring me into this. It's bad enough that I'm stuck here. I'm not baby-sitting a bunch of giggling little girls."

"Nobody's asking you to baby-sit," I said. "It's just that Mom wouldn't worry if she knew you were upstairs. Right, Mom?"

My mother looked from Tom to me and shook her head. "I don't know, Kaitlin. The first time strange girls come to the house and I'm not here? I don't like the sound of that at all."

"Mom—they're not going to set fire to the place or break anything, for pete's sake. They're nice girls. They're my friends, and I really, really want them here."

I remembered what Lexie had said always worked with her mom. "Please? Pretty please with sugar on top?"

Mom was thinking about it, I could tell. "Well . . ." she began.

"We'll be very responsible, and we won't make a mess, and you can definitely trust us," I added. "I'm a middle school student now, after all. You should be giving me more responsibility. You don't want me to be treated like a baby all my life, do you?"

Mom gave a big, deep sigh. "I suppose there can't be any harm in it," she said. "We should be home before eleven and Tom will be here. . . ."

I flung my arms around her neck. "I love you," I said. "I'm going to nominate you for Mother of the Year. We'll be so good—you won't be sorry, I promise."

"I sincerely hope not," she said, laughing nervously. "I don't know what the other girls' mothers will think about this when they find out that we've left you home alone. They won't think we're very responsible parents."

"Mom, Lexie's been—" I was about to say that Lexie had been everywhere and done everything by herself. She even spent weekends with her famous TV cameraman dad when she wasn't with her movie star mom. But I swallowed back the words at the last moment. I'd just been trying to reassure my mother that she had nothing to worry about and that my friends were well brought up little angels like me. If she knew how wild Lexie was, I had a feeling she just might change her mind again.

"Lexie's been what, Kaitlin?"

"Lexie's been dying to see this place, especially Tom's turret room," I said quickly.

Tom poked his head back in through the kitchen door. "Mom, I don't want those kids coming up and pestering me," he said. "I won't get any studying done if they hang around."

"That's right, Kaitlin," Mom said. "You understand you're not to bother Tom at all. And I feel that I should speak to your friends' mothers, just to check that they understand we won't be here to supervise."

I had a horrible vision of Mom and Lexie, meeting on the phone. "I'll call them and make sure they've checked with their mothers," I said. "Middle school students don't get their mothers to call for them."

"Very well, you call them," Mom said.

I ran out to the phone in the front hall. I was kind of scared about calling Lexie. What if her mother answered? I wouldn't know what to say to a movie star—if she really was one. But it was Lexie herself who picked up the phone. "Taylor residence," she said, sounding very grown up. "This is Alexis speaking."

"Lexie, it's Kaitlin. My mom said okay."

"Way to go, KD! Did the 'pretty please with sugar on top' work?"

"Yes, it did." I looked down the hall to see if my mom was in hearing range. "You're a genius."

"See—I knew it would. I'm an expert when it comes to getting what I want out of parents. I'll go pack my stuff. Do you want me to bring any music? I've got some great new CDs."

"I don't have a CD player," I began, then I realized I

was sounding dweebish again, "but there's one down-stairs in the den. We can use that. Oh, and Lexie. My parents are going out to dinner, and my mom wanted to make sure your mother didn't mind that we were going to be alone in the house, except for Tom."

I could hear Lexie laughing through the phone. "That's so funny," she said. "My mom's totally cool about stuff like that. She treats me like an adult, actually. And anyway, I usually go to my dad's on Friday night, and I've already called and told him not to come pick me up until tomorrow. But he wouldn't care, either."

"I didn't think so," I said, "but my mother's a total worrywart, so I had to say it. Can you be here around seven?"

"I can't wait," Lexie said.

"Neither can I."

I put down the phone and called Emily.

"Guess what?" I yelled when Emily answered. "It's okay. You can come."

"Awesome," Emily said. "What time?"

"Seven. My mom wants to meet you and give us instructions before they go out to dinner. And she wants you to check that it's okay with your mom that we're going to be home alone."

"We have the house to ourselves? That's so cool," Emily said. "Why should my mother worry? You'll be there, and so will Lexie, and I even baby-sit my little brother sometimes. So it's not like we're going to have a wild party and wreck the place."

"You see, Mom," I said, sticking my head through the doorway with a triumphant grin on my face.

61

"My friends already baby-sit. They're used to being left alone."

Mom hesitated. "I don't really like it, Kaitlin, but I'm prepared to trust you this once, as long as you can promise me that you'll be mature and responsible."

"I will, Mom," I said. "You can definitely count on me. And my friends are mature and responsible, too. We'll just stay in my room and talk and play board games and—oh, my gosh, look at the time! They'll be here in two hours, and I've got to get everything ready."

I was talking so quickly, I hardly gave my mother a chance to react. She just sat there looking at me, with a worried expression. "I truly promise everything will be fine," I said, and gave my mother another hug for good measure. Then I turned and sprinted up the stairs. I had two hours until Emily and Lexie got here, and I had to give my room a complete makeover.

SEVEN

When I'd had sleepovers before, my mother had arranged most things. She'd baked cookies—low fat, high fiber, of course—and made lemonade or hot chocolate for us. She'd even driven me to the video store to pick out movies to rent. But this sleepover was all mine. I wanted it to be really special—the most exciting sleepover in the history of the universe. I wanted Emily and Lexie to go home saying, "That KD sure is fun to be with!"

But when I looked at my room, I wasn't sure how fun it looked. I had really liked my new room. I liked the window seat and the white lacy curtains. I liked my old-fashioned quilt and my stuffed toys and my braided rug. But now, as I looked at it, I wasn't sure. Suddenly it looked so little-girlish, so juvenile, so boring. On the wall I still had the framed picture of tiger kittens that my great-aunt sent me for my third birthday. I still had all my stuffed animals on a shelf above my bed, and on my dresser was Kayla, Princess of Power.

Let me explain that Kayla, Princess of Power, was really a Barbie. I'd turned her into a superheroine with a magic jewel on her forehead and wristbands that shot out killer beams. She stood on a little trunk that contained a stuffed dragon, some evil action figures that Tom once owned, and a magic wand. I used to play with her all the time long ago, before we moved. In fact, I used to pretend that I was Kayla and I could fly and other dumb stuff like that. I still liked looking at her and knowing that she would watch over me at night with her laser wrists ready, even though I knew I was really too old to play with Barbies now.

But I wasn't sure what my new friends would think about someone who still had Barbies and stuffed animals in her room. I was sure they had posters of rock stars on their walls, like Tom, and they'd only want to do cool stuff, like listen to CDs. Suddenly I wasn't so sure that I wanted the sleepover after all. What if they got bored and decided to go home?

I opened my closet and pulled everything out, trying to see if I had anything that Emily and Lexie might think was fun. I didn't even have a good collection of tapes—only embarrassing, babyish stuff like *Beauty and the Beast* that relatives had bought for my birthdays. My allowance wasn't big enough to buy music that I really wanted. But both Tom and Christine had tons of good music, if I could get my hands on it. There were plenty of board games that I liked to play, but maybe Lexie and Emily would think those were boring, too. Then I realized that we didn't even have anything worth pigging out on in the kitchen. Nobody in the world would want to eat themselves silly on oat bran!

I sprinted into the kitchen and found the instant hot chocolate and a big tub of frozen yogurt in the freezer. That was fine. Frozen yogurt was cool. Even the low-fat cookies tasted okay when dipped in frozen yogurt. At least we wouldn't starve. I ran upstairs again and barely had time to shove everything back into my closet and plump the pillows on my bed before Mom called us to supper.

While Tom and I got stuck loading the dishwasher, Christine disappeared upstairs and then rushed down again, dressed as if she was about to try out for a part on *90210*.

"I thought you were going to a football game," I said to her.

"I am," she said.

"So why are you all dressed up? You'll fall off the bleachers in those high heels."

"Other people might be there, you know," she said.

"There usually is more than one person at a football game," I said.

"Shut up," she snapped. "You wait until you're old enough to notice boys."

"I notice boys," I said, tossing back my hair the way she did. "I'm a sixth grader now, you know." Then I did my grand exit.

I didn't add that most of the boys I noticed were totally disgusting and I wouldn't want to talk to them if they were the last creatures left on earth. But I guessed there might be a few cute ones, here and there. Ryan Sanders was okay, for example.

Tom passed me in the hall as he was heading for

his room. "Oh, well, here I go to solitary confinement. Back to the slammer! Unjust imprisonment," he called out, for Mom's benefit. Then he saw me. "You'd better not bug me unless the house is burning down," he said fiercely. "I've got a whole lot of studying to do if I want to go on that bike ride with my friends in the morning."

"Don't worry," I said. "I wouldn't want to make my friends suffer by having to talk to you. They're used to intelligent people, since they're in the gifted program."

I was grinning to myself as I went back upstairs. Tom and I were now in the same school. We were equals, and I was going to show him that he couldn't push me around anymore.

I changed into my favorite old jeans that are almost ripped in the knee. I wanted to stick my finger in and make them completely ripped, like everyone else's jeans, but I knew my mother. If she saw I was wearing torn clothing, she'd buy me a new pair. But I pulled a few more threads out of the knee as I curled up on the window seat and waited for my friends to arrive.

I jumped as Christine tapped on my door, then stuck her head inside. "Sorry I snapped at you just now," she said. "I'm just upset about this new school. Everyone seems so dorky. I don't know if I'll meet anyone I like."

"You will," I said. "I've met Emily and Lexie."

She grinned. "Good luck with your sleepover tonight. You can borrow my CDs if you're careful with them."

"Thanks," I said. I couldn't believe my luck with everything tonight.

As my sister left, I heard my dad come home. Mom started telling him to hurry up and get changed or they'd be late, and Dad said he'd just spent an hour and a half in stop-and-go traffic and he needed to catch his breath, for pete's sake.

The minutes ticked by very, very slowly. I went between bursting with excitement and worrying that it would be a total disaster. One of the worrying segments had to do with my mother meeting Lexie for the first time. I remembered how speechless Mrs. Bliese had been, and she's a teacher—she must have seen all kinds of unusual sixth graders during her career. What if Mom freaked out and decided that Lexie looked like she might have a rock band hidden in the bushes outside and be a bad influence on her precious little daughter?

I wished I'd thought to suggest to Lexie that she put on her most boring clothes to meet my mother—if Lexie even owned any boring clothes, which I doubted.

I was still trying to decide how to smooth over this first meeting when a bright red convertible screeched to a halt outside our house and Lexie got out. There was a woman with long blond hair driving who had to be Lexie's mother, the "maybe" movie star. Lexie leaned across to give her a kiss on her cheek. I didn't have a chance to see if I recognized Lexie's mom or even if she was beautiful before the car roared off. I ran downstairs, hoping to open the front door before my mother got there. There was an outside chance that I could whisk Lexie upstairs before she ever met my mother—or my mother might be running late for her dinner date and by the time they met, Lexie might be in pj's, looking like anyone else.

No such luck.

"Was that the doorbell?" Mom called, and appeared at her bedroom door, already dressed in her going-out-to-dinner outfit, complete with pearls.

"It's okay, it's Lexie," I said, but Mom came downstairs anyway.

I took a deep breath, closed my eyes, and opened the door.

"Hey, KD, how's it going?" Lexie said, and swept past me into the house. "Hi, you must be KD's mother. I'm Alexis Taylor."

Slowly I opened my eyes again. Lexie was holding out her hand to my mother. My mother was shaking it and actually smiling. "Very nice to meet you, Alexis," she was saying. "Kaitlin's done nothing but talk about you all week."

I couldn't believe it. Lexie's mop of wild curls was tied back in a ponytail, and she was wearing purple sweatpants and a large baseball shirt over a white long-sleeved T-shirt. She looked completely ordinary and very un-Lexie-like.

"Why don't you help Alexis take her things up to your room, Kaitlin?" my mother said.

"You can call me Lexie if you like, Mrs. Durham," Lexie said.

"All right, Lexie," Mom said. She was still smiling.

"Is that a British accent?" Lexie asked sweetly. I held my breath again.

"Yes, it is. I grew up in England," Mom said.

"I love London," Lexie said. "It's one of my favorite cities."

"You've been to England? How nice," Mom said. She sounded impressed. "We must talk about it when I have more time, but right now my husband and I have a dinner engagement, and I don't think Kaitlin would want me stealing her new friend—would you, sweetie pie?"

Lexie hadn't been kidding when she said she knew the way to handle parents. She was an expert.

Before Lexie and I could head upstairs, Emily arrived in a truck with Thumbelina Horse Ranch written on the side.

Before I could stop her, Mom had gone out to meet the truck, obviously to reassure Emily's mother that she wasn't a terrible parent for leaving us alone. Lexie and Emily and I danced around the front hall excitedly.

"Heavens above," my mother said as she came back in. "You'd have thought you girls hadn't seen each other for weeks from the amount of noise you're making."

"Come on up to my room," I said, taking the stairs two at a time.

"All right, girls, jog up the stairs. Lift those feet. One-two, one-two. We'll soon have you whipped into shape," Lexie said, giving a perfect imitation of Mr. Meany's voice.

"Which room?" Lexie asked.

"This one." I pushed open my door and stepped back to let them go in ahead of me.

"Kaitlin, it's so pretty—just like I thought it would be," Emily exclaimed.

"Nice," Lexie said, walking around and examining everything.

I just stood there holding my breath. My friends actually seemed to like my room! All the same, I was waiting for Lexie to say something about the babyish posters on the wall. She got as far as the stuffed animals, then she stopped, staring at them.

"Way to go, KD," she said. "So you're into endangered species, too."

"What?"

"All these animals—you've collected them because they're endangered, right? The leopard and the whale and those adorable little tiger cubs . . . all on the endangered list. I'm crazy about animals myself, especially endangered ones."

"Oh, sure. Endangered species," I said, and gave her what I hoped was a convincing smile.

"All my pets are pretty close to being endangered species," Lexie said carelessly. "That's why I keep them."

"What sort of pets?" I asked. I could only think of gerbils and hamsters, aside from dogs and cats.

"Let's see," she said. "There's the desert tortoise. He's very endangered. And the iguana . . ."

"You have an iguana?"

"Of course," she said in a way that sounded like, "Doesn't everybody?"

She dumped her bag down on my bed. "He's very intelligent," she said. "Do you have any pets?"

"Not yet. But my parents promised we could get a dog when we got settled. There wasn't any room in the city."

"How about you, Emily?"

"You name it, we've got it," Emily said. "Horses, dogs, cats, chickens, pygmy goats . . . great for someone with allergies like me." She made a face.

"You should get a boa constrictor, like me," Lexie said. "He's totally hypoallergenic."

"A boa constrictor? You're kidding, right?" I squeaked.

Lexie gave me a funny look. "What's wrong with a boa constrictor?"

"Nothing, except they grow to twenty feet long and crush you to death and then swallow you."

Lexie shook her head so that all her curls danced in the ponytail. "Norman's not that big yet, and he'd never crush me. We're best friends," she said.

She gave me a big smile. Right, I thought. This was another of her stories, like the movie star mother and Emily's twenty-four-inch horses.

"What's this, KD?" Emily asked.

She was holding Kayla, Princess of Power.

"You still play with Barbies?" Lexie asked.

"Of course I don't," I said hastily. I could feel my cheeks getting hot. "I just keep her there to look at, because I was kind of proud of the way I designed her costume."

"You made that costume yourself?" Emily sounded impressed.

I nodded.

"You are so talented," she said. "What's she supposed to be?"

"She's Kayla, Princess of Power."

"Who?"

"A female superhero. I invented her. My brother had all these superhero action figures when he was a little kid and I wanted one, too, so I invented Kayla. She fights against evil. The wristbands send out paralyzing rays, and the jewel on her head lets her see into people's minds far away. Oh, and she can fly."

I stopped, feeling stupid. I was sure they were going to laugh.

"Interesting," Lexie said. "Who does she fight?"

"Evil creatures," I said. "I've got them in the case."

Lexie grabbed the case and opened it. "Ooh, he's ugly," she said, taking out one of the figures. Then she grabbed another. "And this one is Mr. Meany." It was an old Wrestlemania figure, complete with bulging muscles.

Lexie took Kayla from Emily. "At last Mr. Meany meets his doom. Kayla, Princess of Power, goes to the gym with her death rays. She zaps Mr. Meany and he flies across the room. . . ." She threw the figure. It landed on the carpet and rolled underneath the bed.

"Take that, you evil creature," Lexie said. Emily scrambled under the bed and found the figure. "But Mr. Meany is in good physical shape," she yelled, waving the figure at Lexie. "The death rays didn't work against those muscles."

"So she takes over his mind, and she makes him

run around the edge of the school," Lexie went on. "Around and around in the heat until he goes mad with exhaustion and she says . . ."

"Now you can do a hundred sit-ups," I chimed in. We were all laughing pretty hard by now.

"But Mr. Meany climbs the rope to get away," Emily yelled, leaping onto my bed and putting the doll on my top shelf.

"And Kayla flies after him. 'You think you can get away from Kayla, Princess of Power, human weakling? Take that and that!' He falls from the top of the rope and . . . splat."

"He lands on top of Pee Wee Pugh!" Emily finished for her.

Now we had totally lost it. We lay on my bed with tears coming out of our eyes. We didn't even hear the knock on my door and when it opened, we leaped up guiltily as if we'd been doing something wrong.

We all looked up as my mother's, then my father's face appeared around the door.

"Is something the matter, girls?" my mother asked, looking at Emily's red face and the tears running down my cheeks.

"We were playing Barbies, Mrs. Durham," Lexie said sweetly, making us all start giggling again.

"Do you want to introduce me to your friends, Kaitlin?" Dad said.

I got control of myself. "Sure, Dad. This is Lexie, and this is Emily. This is my dad," I said. It sounded stupid when I said it. After all, who else would he be, standing next to my mother in our house?

"Hello, girls," Dad said. He shook hands with them. "I'm sorry we have to leave you alone like this, but we have an important dinner engagement. It's with a business contact of mine."

"A business contact?" Lexie said, her eyes opening very wide. "Oh, right. I get it. A restaurant would be a good place to meet your . . . contacts. I mean, nobody notices what goes on at other tables in a restaurant, do they?"

For a second I looked as confused as my father did. Then suddenly it hit me. I remembered all that dumb stuff I'd made up about spies and the CIA. I felt a cold jolt go all the way up my spine. How could I have done something so stupid? Any second now, Lexie was going to put her foot in it and I was going to look like a total fool. My father was looking at her as if she might not have all her marbles.

My dad coughed at the back of his throat, something he always did when he wasn't quite sure of what to say. "We're actually having dinner with an ex-colleague of mine who now works for another branch of the bank," he said.

"Oh, right," Lexie said, giving Emily and me a knowing look. "Works for another branch. Don't worry, we understand."

"Lexie!" I hissed, and shook my head in warning.

"Oh, sorry," Lexie said. "I forgot."

My father still had that surprised look on his face that Mrs. Bliese had when she first laid eyes on Lexie. "Forgot what?" my dad asked.

"Nothing," Lexie said. "Forget I even mentioned it. It's okay. I don't know anything, really. Just forget about it."

My father gave me a look to tell me he thought my friends might be a little strange. Then he pulled himself together. "Okay, girls, listen up. Some last-minute things," he said. "I've written the number of the restaurant on the message board by the phone. If there's a real emergency, you know to dial 911, don't you? And Tom's upstairs, but don't disturb him unless you really have to."

"Okay, Dad," I said. "We'll be fine."

"And you know about not trying to cook anything when we're not here," my mother added, "and the neighbors' numbers are on the message board, too, and don't answer the front door without knowing who is out there, and if the phone rings don't tell strangers that we're not home. Just say we can't come to the phone right now—"

"Mom, we'll be fine," I interrupted. Any second now she'd be reminding me to brush my teeth before I went to bed.

"Oh, and don't forget to brush your teeth before you go to bed," she added.

"Would you please go?" I snapped. Talk about humiliating!

"We're just trying to make sure we've taken care of everything," my father said firmly. I could tell he wasn't happy about my tone of voice. "Have a good time, girls, and don't get into any mischief."

"We won't," we all said at the same time.

We heard them go down the stairs and then the front door slammed and the car started up in the driveway.

Lexie climbed onto the window seat. "They've gone," she yelled. "We're all alone. We've got the whole house to ourselves. It's party time! Hooray!"

EIGHT

I don't know why we went so crazy. I mean, what was so incredible about having the house to ourselves? It's just that we seemed to think so at the time. We danced and leaped around my room, yelling, "We're alone, we're free. Now's the time to par-tee!" until I remembered one minor detail.

"Quiet, guys. Chill," I said, grabbing Lexie as she danced by me.

"What?"

"We're not exactly home alone."

"Why not?"

"My brother's up in his room," I said, lowering my voice. "He's studying up there. I'm not supposed to disturb him."

"You mean we can't even look into the turret room?" Emily said.

"Sure we can, but later," I said.

"Later's okay," Lexie said. "It will be spookier up there when it's really dark."

"What's he doing up there that can't be disturbed?" Emily asked.

"Studying."

"Studying already? We've only been in school a week."

"He flunked his math placement. He got put into intro to math."

"You mean math for very stupid people?" Lexie asked, grinning.

"That's not nice—" Emily began, but I nodded. "Yeah, math for stupid people, and my parents are really mad," I said. "He has to retake the test on Monday. He did badly because he was goofing off. He's really smart, but he thought it would be kind of neat to be in a math class where you got to build pyramids from sugar cubes."

"Sounds okay to me," Emily said. "I have to start on equations and X and Y. I don't like the sound of it."

"You'll ace it," Lexie said. "But we should let your brother study, KD. How about we go downstairs and put on some music?"

"Sure. My sister has a lot of good CDs. She said we could borrow them."

I led them into Christine's room. We climbed over the mountains of clothes on her floor and found her shelf of CDs.

"Boy, your sister has a lot of clothes," Emily said.

"She worked last summer, and she's done a lot of baby-sitting," I said. "My mom would never buy them for her, so she buys her own clothes. And her own music. I can't wait until I'm old enough."

"Is she out on a date tonight?"

"She went to the football game and then out for

78

pizza," I said. "I don't know who with, but she certainly took a lot of time getting dressed. She must have tried on a zillion outfits. Mom would never have let her leave everything all over the place if she'd seen her room like this."

"I can't wait until we're old enough to go to football games and out for pizza afterward," Emily said with a sigh.

"I've been to hundreds of football games. They're okay, I guess," Lexie said.

"But it's different when it's your own school team and everyone's cheering," I said in agreement with Emily.

Lexie made a face. "Don't tell me you'd like to be a cheerleader?"

"I might," I said, blushing because of the fierce way she was looking at me. "I've taken years of ballet."

"KD, cheerleading is so sexist," Lexie said. "Boys play sports and girls get to cheer them on. Is that right?"

"I guess not," I said. I'd never really thought about it before, but it did seem strange, the way Lexie put it.

She was grabbing CDs from the shelf. "Hey, she's got a lot of good classic stuff here. The Who—I love that band. And the Stones."

We went into the family room and spread all the CDs out on the rug. "Put the Stones on first," Lexie said. "Don't you think they're great? They're so loud. The neighbors always complain if I play their music at home. We live in a condo and we've got thin walls."

As I put the CD into the player, I made a mental note that I'd been right all along. If Lexie's mother really was a movie star, they wouldn't live in a condo with thin walls, would they? They'd have a mansion.

The deep bass thump and the wail of guitars filled the room. It wasn't the sort of music you could just sit and listen to. You had to do something. We started to play air guitar along with the music. Emily sat on the arm of the sofa and pretended to play drums. Then Lexie picked up the TV remote control and mouthed the words into it like a microphone. It was hard to keep it up because we were laughing so hard.

Then the next number started. It had a really strong beat and Lexie started to dance. "Come on," she shouted.

We joined her.

"Too bad there aren't any boys here. We could have a party," she said.

"I don't know any boys I'd want to dance with," Emily said.

"Can you imagine dancing with Pee Wee Pugh?" I shrieked.

"Yuck, gross," she said. "The whole room would vibrate when he danced. And he'd probably make his animal noises in time to the beat."

We started to giggle.

"I can't imagine dancing with any sixth-grade boys," I said.

"Most of them are such little shrimps," Emily said. "Can you imagine slow dancing with them? How embarrassing!"

"They'd only come up to my shoulder," Lexie yelled, laughing. "But don't forget, we have middle school dances now. We might get to dance with seventh graders, and there are some very cute eighth graders."

"Yeah, right," I said. "Can you see any eighth grader with normal vision wanting to dance with us?"

"What's wrong with us?" Lexie demanded. "I'd say we were three gorgeous babes."

For some reason Emily and I found this funny. We couldn't stand up to dance anymore.

"Anyway, I can't go to a school dance," I said. "I don't even know any real dance steps. I only know what I've seen on TV. Someone will have to teach me before the first school dance."

"It's simple." Lexie was moving to the music, her arms flying out and her body shaking. "We used to dance at parties in L.A."

"I don't know," Emily said. "It might be simple for you. But I've tried dancing like I see on TV and I look like a robot out of control. I can't get my arms and legs to move at the same time or in the same direction."

"Okay, try this," Lexie said. "Go step-and-sway, step-and-sway, and then move your arms like this." She showed us and we followed along. "Great," she said. "See, you've got it. Now move your shoulders like this and add another step. Hey, girls, we're getting good! We're so good, we're bad! Now you're moving, now we're cool . . ."

"We're the coolest in the school!" I joined in.

We got into this routine, all moving together. "Now we're moving, now we're cool. We're the coolest in the school," we chanted.

We linked arms and turned into something like a

chorus line, kicking up our legs wildly. We were doing great until Lexie and I moved to the right just as Emily swung to the left.

"Whoa," Lexie yelled as Emily fell to the floor, dragging me with her. One minute we were dancing, the next we were in a tangled heap on the floor. Not just the floor but the bare wood part, not the part with the rug. We skidded across the parquet and into a big lamp. The lamp teetered and then toppled over with a dramatic crash.

"Oh no," Emily wailed.

"Is it okay?" Lexie asked as I scrambled to my feet and tried to pick up the lamp. "It wasn't a family heirloom or anything, was it?"

I didn't think it was a family heirloom, but then, I didn't think my folks would be too pleased if they came home to a busted lamp after my first sleepover with my new friends. Somehow we all got it upright again. I turned the switch and . . . the light came on. We all cheered.

"Maybe we should be a little more careful," Emily suggested. "No more of Lexie's wild dances."

"Maybe we're not cut out to be singular sensations," Lexie said with a grin.

We flopped down on the sofa.

"Your brother sure must be studying hard," Lexie said. "We were kind of loud, weren't we?"

Now that she mentioned it, I was kind of surprised myself. It would have been just like Tom to come stomping down the stairs, telling us that we were disturbing him.

"I'm pooped," Emily said. "Let's get something to drink."

I led the way through to the kitchen and poured lemonade.

Lexie was opening cabinets. "What have you got to eat that's good?"

"It depends on what you think is good," I said. "My mother doesn't go in for junk food. We've got homemade cookies and frozen yogurt—"

"Popcorn," Emily yelled, picking up an unopened bag. "I just love popcorn."

"Okay, we'll have popcorn," I said.

Lexie examined it. "It's not microwave. Do you have a popper?"

"We must somewhere." I started looking among the appliances. I knew what it looked like, although I'd never actually used it. I found it and put it on the counter.

"How does it work?" Lexie asked. "Do you know how to use it? It looks kind of old-fashioned. We have an air popper at home."

"It's simple," I said. There weren't any directions with it, but what could be hard about making popcorn? I'd seen my mother do it hundreds of times.

"We need to put some oil in the bottom," I said, "or it won't pop right."

Trying to look like a person who makes popcorn every day, I plugged the popper in, poured in some oil, and then poured some popcorn kernels on top of the oil.

"Put in plenty," Emily said. "I *love* popcorn."

I poured in more. The popper was still less than half full.

"Maybe I should put in the whole package," I suggested.

"Yeah, go ahead. We need enough to keep us going all night," Lexie said.

I poured the whole bagful in and put on the lid. "Okay. We'll hear when it starts popping," I said. "Do you guys want to listen to more music?"

"Let's see what's on TV," Lexie said. "Maybe there's a good movie, and we can curl up and eat popcorn. I just love doing that."

We went back into the family room and turned on the TV. I started flicking through the channels.

"And now back to our movie, *Nightmare on Elm Street, Part Ten*," the announcer was saying.

"Wait, hold it," Lexie yelled. "*Nightmare on Elm Street, Part Ten?* That's perfect. Let's watch it. You know—that's the one with the zombies who come out of the ground. I love that one, don't you?"

"I never saw it." I couldn't tell her that I wasn't allowed to watch movies like that or, worse still, that I was scared to watch movies like that. Emily didn't seem to think there was anything wrong with it.

"We need a quilt to snuggle up under," she said.

"I'll go get KD's quilt," Lexie said, and bounded up the stairs. I sat down next to Emily and wondered if I should say something to her about being scared of horror movies. Maybe she felt that way, too. Maybe she was only trying to act brave.

84

"This is going to be fun," she said, giving me a big smile. Okay, so that killed that little idea. . . .

I felt as if there was a big lump in my throat. My heart was hammering as the scary music started coming from the TV.

"Don't think there is any way of escape," a spooky voice was saying. "We have come for your soul. . . ."

I didn't know how to get out of this without looking like a baby. Besides being scared to death, I was feeling guilty because I knew what my parents would say if they knew I was making something in the kitchen and watching a horror movie. I'd be in big trouble if we were still watching when they came home. But maybe I'd already have died from heart failure by then, so it wouldn't matter.

Lexie came down with the quilt, and we wrapped it around us as we sat on the sofa. A young girl was awakened by tapping on her window. In the cemetery next door the graves were moving, and horrible creatures with blank stares were coming out of the ground, walking toward the girl's room with their arms stretched out. She was too scared to go to the window. The tapping got louder. "We have come for your soul," the voices chanted, and then suddenly . . .

There was an awful exploding noise. It sounded like someone was shooting bullets in the next room. For a second we were too scared to move.

Emily grabbed me, screaming, "Zombies! They're here!"

I think I was screaming, too. I know my mouth was

85

open, and I think that sound was coming out. I was too scared to notice.

Then we all realized what it was at the same moment. "The popcorn!" We jumped up and ran into the kitchen. The lid had flown off the popcorn popper and popcorn was flying in all directions. Some pieces were bouncing off the ceiling, some were hitting the cabinets or pinging against the pots and pans, and some came flying out the door into our faces.

"Zombies have got the popcorn popper!" Emily wailed.

I ran in and unplugged the popper. It was almost empty now—the only place in the kitchen not covered in popcorn.

"I think we might have put in too much, you guys," Lexie said in a quavering voice. For a moment I thought she was about to cry, but then I saw that she was about to burst out laughing. She picked up the bag from the wastebasket. "Maybe we should have read the directions first."

"What does it say?" I peered over her shoulder.

"It says put in one level measure of popcorn," Emily read.

"One measure? You mean like this?" Lexie held up a plastic scooper that had been in the bag with the popcorn. It was the size of a teaspoon. None of us had noticed it.

We looked at each other, not knowing whether to laugh or cry. "No wonder it's all over the walls," Lexie said.

"And the ceiling," I added.

"You know what, guys? I think we've got some cleaning up to do," Emily said seriously.

"No, really? I thought we'd just lie on the floor and eat our way across," Lexie said.

Now we really lost it. It was so terrible and so funny and so scary at the same time. We sat down on the popcorn-covered floor and laughed until the tears ran down our cheeks.

NINE

It didn't take as long as I'd hoped to clear up the invasion of the killer popcorn. I'd realized pretty early on in the cleanup process that this would be a great way to get out of watching a movie I didn't want to watch. But my friends were being way too efficient. Emily went around the counters with a bowl saying, "We can save this piece. This piece is okay."

Lexie stood on a step stool on top of a kitchen chair with a broom in her hand, swaying dangerously and making swipes at the ceiling to wipe off the oily marks and bits of corn still stuck there. I started sweeping popcorn off the floor and getting rid of it down the garbage disposal.

Every second I expected to see Tom peek around the kitchen door, saying, "What're you doing? Mom's going to be so mad!" Sound obviously didn't travel all the way up to the turret room, I guessed.

By the time we'd finished, we were just in time for the most scary part of the movie. The zombies had taken over the girl's boyfriend, and she was letting him into the house, not knowing that he was now one of the zombies and he'd come for her. I just couldn't watch. My heart was thudding so loudly that the other two must have heard it. I wished I could have brought down Kayla, Princess of Power, to protect me.

"So, Scott, what do you want to do tonight?" the girl was asking. Didn't she notice that his eyes had gotten weird? I wouldn't have let in a guy whose eyes kept glowing red and green!

"Do tonight? Can't you guess, Susan?" Even his voice was weird. She was totally dumb. *Run away, Susan. Get out of there*, I wanted to shout. I couldn't stand it. If I could pretend I was cold, I could bring the quilt up over my face and I wouldn't have to watch. . . .

"Gee, it's cold in here," I said. "I'm glad we've got the quilt to snuggle under."

I'd done it. The quilt was over my head. It shut out some of Susan's screams, too. I screwed up my eyes tight and tried to cover my ears as the scary music reached its climax. When I finally dared peek out again, the credits were rolling up the screen. I looked around and saw that Emily and Lexie were just peeking out, too.

"You guys hid under the covers, too," I yelled, happy that I wasn't the only chicken in the universe.

"I just got cold," Lexie said.

Emily and I looked at each other and grinned.

"You think I was scared of a dumb little horror movie?" Lexie demanded. "I've seen hundreds of them. I've even seen a horror movie being made. It's only actors in costume, you know. And it's not real

89

blood. Don't tell me you two were scared?" She gave a fake laugh. "That's so funny."

Shut up, I wanted to say. I went to poke her in the side, but instead of Lexie's side, my hand touched something weird—something rough and furry and bumpy. I screamed.

"What?" Emily shrieked.

"There's something under here," I said shakily. I tried to pull back the quilt.

"Wait, don't pull that back—I'm cold," Lexie said, tugging on the quilt.

"But there's something weird under here," I said. I flung off the quilt. Emily pounced on the object. "It's an old stuffed animal," she said. "Did you bring it down by mistake with the quilt from KD's room?"

"It's not mine," I said. "I've never seen it before."

Lexie snatched it up. "If you really want to know, it's Barnaby Bunny," she said angrily.

"Barnaby Bunny?" Emily and I looked at each other and grinned.

"My stuffed rabbit. He goes everywhere with me. I can't sleep without him."

Emily and I started to giggle. "And you pretended you weren't scared of the movie," Emily said. "But you had to bring down your toy rabbit so you wouldn't be afraid."

Lexie snatched up Barnaby Bunny. "I'm going to bed," she said, and stalked off upstairs.

Emily and I sat there looking at each other. I got up and turned off the TV. Emily picked up the quilt.

"I guess we should go up and say we're sorry," she said.

"She was mean to us first," I said. "She made fun of us for being scared."

"I know," Emily said. "But I get the feeling that Lexie is the kind of person who doesn't ever want people to know what she's really like inside."

I nodded. "Okay. Let's talk to her. I hope she won't stay mad at us."

"Me, too. I really like her, even if she is weird sometimes."

"Me, too. We sort of go together, like a sandwich."

Emily grinned. "We're the bread and she's the peanut butter."

We gathered up Christine's CDs and put them back in her room. Then we went into my bedroom, carrying the rest of the popcorn. Lexie was lying on her sleeping bag, staring at the ceiling. Barnaby Bunny was in her arms.

"We're sorry we laughed at you," I said. "It's okay to have stuffed animals. I've got a bunch."

Lexie kept on staring at the ceiling. "You guys made fun of me," she said. "I thought you were my friends. I hate being teased."

"You laughed at us first. You made us feel bad," Emily said.

"That was different."

"No, it wasn't," I said. "We were feeling scared, and you acted like you were better than us. That wasn't nice. If you were our friend, you'd have admitted you were scared. We could have all laughed together."

91

"And it was pretty funny," Emily said slowly. "All three of us with the quilt over our heads. Nobody was watching the movie."

"It was a dumb movie anyway," Lexie growled. "Not worth watching. That girl was so stupid. Didn't she see that her boyfriend had turned into a zombie?"

"That's what I thought," I said. "It was totally obvious."

"I thought so, too," Emily agreed.

Lexie sat up. "You won't tell anyone at school about Barnaby Bunny, will you?"

"Of course not," Emily and I said together.

Lexie hugged him to her. "I know it's babyish to have a stuffed rabbit at our age, but I've sort of gotten used to having him with me. When I was little and I went between my mother's house and my dad's house and my grandma's house, he was the only thing that came with me everywhere. Now I can't sleep without him."

"We understand," Emily said.

"Sure," I added.

Lexie got up and put Barnaby Bunny on my bed. "That movie was pretty scary," she admitted. "Especially because it was about a girl in a house alone and zombies tapping on the window, and now we're here alone. . . ."

We looked at one another. It had just begun to sink in that we were here alone. Then we all remembered Tom at the same moment.

"We still haven't seen the turret room," Lexie said. "Now might be a good time to go visit your brother."

"He might be getting hungry, and we could bring him the rest of the popcorn," Emily added.

"Great idea," I said.

We all scrambled for the door together. I led the way to the end of the hall and up the little staircase that went to Tom's room. It was dark and spooky even when I turned on the light and the boards creaked under our feet. Tom's door was closed.

"It's very quiet in there. You don't think he's already asleep, do you?" Emily asked.

"Tom, asleep at ten o'clock? That would be a first." But Tom studying with no music blasting away was also a first. I tapped lightly on the door.

"Tom? Can we come in for a second?"

No answer.

We looked at one another, and then I turned the doorknob. The door opened with a squeaking sound, just like in the horror movie. Tom's desk lamp was on. His books were open on his desk, but there was no sign of him.

"Tom? Are you in here?"

We went in cautiously. His window was open, and the lace curtains were flapping in the wind. The air coming in was very cold and was stirring up the papers on his desk. The whole scene was very spooky.

"Tom?" we called. "Tom, where are you? Are you here?"

No answer.

"He might be downstairs, getting a snack," Emily suggested.

"He wouldn't have passed my room without saying

something, even if it was something insulting," I said. "Plus, we would have heard him."

We ran down the stairs and searched everywhere.

"He's not in the house," Lexie said at last.

"You don't think he was taken by zombies?" Emily asked.

"Get real, Emily. It was only actors in costume," Lexie said, but she looked kind of scared, too.

Then I realized that I had the answer and it wasn't zombies.

"I'll bet he sneaked out to go to that party," I said. "He really wanted to go, but Mom and Dad wouldn't let him. Boy, is he going to get it if they find out."

"Are you going to tell them?" Lexie asked.

I shook my head. "He might be a pain, but we don't tell on each other. When you have parents like ours, you have to stick together."

"I think that was mean of him, leaving us all alone," Emily said.

We stood there, looking at each other. Emily's eyes were the size of saucers. We really, truly were home alone in a dark, windy, spooky old house!

"I thought we wanted to be alone, guys," Lexie tried to say in her brightest voice as we headed back to my room. "The whole house to ourselves."

"You guys can explore the turret room now if you like," I said, trying to sound as calm as Lexie. "Don't let me stop you."

"Are you crazy?" Emily said. "I'm not going back up to that room."

"I don't feel like it right now, either," Lexie

said. "That movie and the popcorn have gotten me spooked."

"What time are your folks coming back?" Emily asked.

"Around eleven, they said."

Emily looked at her watch. "It's not even ten thirty yet."

"Listen to that wind. It sounds like a storm's coming," Lexie said. We went across to the window and knelt on the window seat, looking out. It was certainly getting stormy. Tree branches were throwing crazy shadows across the street as they swayed in the wind.

"What's that?" Emily whispered, grabbing my arm.

We listened. Tap tap. Tap tap.

"It's only the tree outside Tom's window brushing against the house," I said, but I heard my voice shake. It did sound like bony fingers. The wind was making sounds I hadn't heard in this house before. *Whooooo*, it whispered through the roof.

"Is this spooky enough for you, Lexie?" Emily tried to joke.

"Spooky enough," Lexie said. "I was just noticing how dark it is on your street, KD. There's only one streetlight, and it's hidden behind the tree. And there are no lights in the other houses. Doesn't anyone live there?"

"Yes, but two old couples live in the houses across from us. They must go to bed early," I said. I was really noticing how dark it was.

Then I felt my heart do a flip-flop. I blinked and

95

looked again. No, I hadn't imagined it—a shape was creeping through our bushes.

"Did you see that?"

"What?"

Emily and Lexie peered out the window on either side of me.

"I thought I saw a shadow move—right there, between those bushes."

"Probably just a cat," Lexie said.

"It was bigger than a cat."

"It could have just been the wind making the bushes move," Emily said.

"No, it wasn't. It dodged."

"There. I saw it," Lexie whispered. She was clutching me now. "Someone's moving in the bushes down there."

"Do you think it's burglars? Maybe they saw your parents go out and they know it's only us here," Emily muttered.

"I'll bet I know what it is," Lexie said.

"What?"

"I'll bet it has something to do with KD's dad—you know, his job as a spy? Maybe some terrorists have found out where he lives . . ."

"And they've been watching the house, and they know he's out to dinner with his spy friends," Emily wailed, "and when Kaitlin's parents come back, there'll be a blast of machine gun fire or they'll blow up the house."

"Shut up, you guys," I said, because they both looked really, really scared now. "That's so silly. There are no terrorists."

"How do you know?" Lexie exclaimed. "Maybe they have a contract out to get rid of your father."

"Quick, call the cops," Emily said, jumping down from my window seat and heading for my door before I could stop her.

"The FBI, Emily," Lexie yelled, running after her. "Or the CIA. How do you find the number for the CIA? Are they in the phone book?"

"Emily, Lexie, wait, listen," I yelled, grabbing them just in time. "There aren't any terrorists. I made it up about my father being a spy. He really works in a bank."

"Why?" Emily asked.

"Why did I make it up or why does he work in a bank?"

"You know what I mean. Why did you lie to us?"

"Because you were both lying to me."

"About what?"

"You know."

Lexie stepped in between us. "Chill out, you guys. It doesn't matter what she told us because someone really is trying to get into this house. I saw the shadow disappear right under KD's room."

"You think we should call the police?" I asked shakily.

"I really do."

"So do I."

"Okay, the phone's downstairs in the hallway. Let's all go together," I said.

I opened my door, and we stepped very quietly into the hall.

We'd gone only a couple of steps when Lexie grabbed Emily and me. "Listen to that!" she hissed.

She didn't have to say anything more. We'd both heard. There were noises downstairs, and they weren't trees tapping on windows this time. They were heavy sounds, as if someone was forcing open a window. Someone was definitely trying to break in, or maybe had already gotten inside. The thumps and bumps were pretty loud and very close.

We rushed back to my room again.

"Quick, push your chest of drawers against the door," Lexie said. "We'll be safe in here."

We struggled with my heavy dresser.

"The burglar will hear us," I said. "He might come up to see what's happening."

"Doesn't matter. At least he won't be able to get in."

"He might have something to break down the door," Emily whispered.

"Shut up. If we can keep him out for a little while, KD's parents will be home."

That was slightly comforting, although I didn't think that our chances would be too great against large, fierce, and heavily armed burglars for half an hour. If only the chest of drawers really did keep the door shut.

"Listen," Emily whispered. "Someone's coming."

Heavy feet were coming up the stairs.

"Quick. Into my closet," I said. "He might not look in there."

We leaped into my closet and closed the door.

"Don't shut it completely. I hate the dark," Lexie

whispered. "And I need to get Barnaby Bunny."

"Forget Barnaby Bunny. We're not opening this door again," I told her.

Even in the closet we could hear the sound of slow, heavy footsteps, coming closer and closer. They got to my door and stopped. It was like my worst nightmare coming true. I was holding my breath. I think the others were, too. I couldn't hear a single sound in the closet.

Suddenly we heard the doorknob turn. Then we heard the sound of a chest being pushed across the floor. He was in the room! I was too scared to scream now, too scared even to blink. The dark shadow came closer and closer.

Then slowly the closet door began to open.

"I know you're in there," said a deep, scary voice.

I opened my mouth to scream, but then I recognized the voice.

"Tom," I yelled. "It's my brother. It's Tom."

"Yes, it's Tom," the voice went on, "but not the Tom you used to know, before he was taken. . . ."

The door opened completely, and my brother was standing in front of us with his arms outstretched. His eyes stared blankly and glowed a strange, sickly green—just like in the movie. "Yes, Kaitlin, I'm a zombie now. And I've come back for you," he said.

As he lunged at us, we screamed so loudly I was sure we could be heard across the street.

TEN

Tom flung himself backward onto my bed, slapping his hands against his thighs as he shook with laughter. "You should see your faces," he shrieked. "I can't believe you guys actually fell for it! You really believed I was a zombie."

"It's not funny, Tom," I shouted. I was that close to exploding. We'd had too many weird things happen to us that night for me to stay cool any longer. "We were really scared. We saw that scary movie, and then we found out that you'd sneaked out without telling Mom and Dad, and we were in the house alone."

"I know," he said, still rocking back and forth as he laughed. "I peeked downstairs before I went out. I saw you watching the movie. I knew you'd flip out. Then when I came back, I heard you screaming about burglars and zombies. It was too perfect."

"So that was you stomping around downstairs?" Lexie demanded.

"Of course, who did you think it was—a burglar?"

"It could have been," I said quickly, before Emily or Lexie could say anything about terrorists.

100

"I climbed out my window," Tom said. "But it wasn't so easy to climb back up again in the dark, with that tree swaying around in the wind, so I tried the down-stairs-bathroom window. It doesn't shut completely. And I remembered that we had those glow-in-the-dark stickers in the family room, so I put one under each eye. Looked pretty good, didn't it? I sure fooled you guys."

"I think you're mean, and you're going to be in big trouble when Mom and Dad find out."

"Hey, come on," Tom said, sitting up now. "It was a joke. A harmless joke. You're not going to tell them I went to the party, are you? It was only for a few seconds."

"Give me just one good reason why I shouldn't tell them everything," I demanded. "You'd be grounded forever and ever. You'll still be grounded when you go and live in a nursing home when you're ninety-nine. Then maybe you might learn not to be mean to me all the time."

"Fine, go ahead, tell them," Tom said quietly. "Then, of course, they'll want to know why you were so freaked out about zombies, and you can tell them you were watching a horror movie on TV. Or making popcorn. I could tell them for you. . . ."

He grinned that annoying, superior grin that al-ways made me want to hit him. "Well, I'm off to bed. It's been a tiring day with all that studying. Sleep well, kiddie-pies. Don't let the zombies get you!"

He started laughing again as he walked down the hall.

"One day I'm going to get even with you, Tom

101

Durham," I yelled after him. "I'll get even with you if it's the last thing I do!"

"In your dreams," he yelled back. "It takes a great brain to outsmart Thomas B. Durham."

"He is so conceited," Lexie commented as I shut my door. "We really should teach that boy a lesson."

"Yes, but how?" I asked, sinking down onto the bed beside her. "He's got us trapped. If I tell on him, he can always tell Mom that I was watching a horror movie, and maybe I won't be allowed to have any more sleepovers."

"Maybe Emily's great brain can come up with something," Lexie said. "Have you got any ideas, ED?"

"Not off the top of my head, but I'll definitely work on it. I want to teach him a lesson for Kaitlin's sake."

"Do your best, Emily. I'd love to show him that I'm not a little kid who can be pushed around all the time."

"I'm going to bed," Lexie said. "After all that excitement, I'm exhausted."

"Me, too," Emily said, yawning. "Maybe I'll save my serious thinking for the morning."

"And your folks will be back soon," Lexie added. "Maybe they'll think we're little angels if we're already in bed . . . and maybe they won't think to look at the kitchen ceiling and see the popcorn stains."

We undressed and brushed our teeth. It felt reassuring to be doing something normal. I hadn't gotten over all the scares of the night. My heart was still racing a mile a minute. For once I was actually looking forward to having my parents come home.

"I don't know if I'll be able to sleep," I said. "I'm still so wound up."

"What a night," Emily said as she wriggled into her sleeping bag. "This definitely was not your normal sleepover. I wonder if all our sleepovers are going to be so action packed."

"I hope not," I said. "At least not the ones at my house."

"I don't know—it was kind of fun," Lexie said. "More exciting than playing Truth or Dare, or calling boys or pigging out."

"I think I'd rather play Truth or Dare and pig out next time," I said. "How about you, Emily?"

Her eyes were shut. "Emily, are you asleep or thinking?"

"Thinking."

"It's okay. You can rest your great brain tonight. We'll think how to get even with Tom in the morning."

"I wasn't thinking about that," Emily said. "I was thinking about the terrorists and the CIA. What did you mean when you said we'd lied to you?"

"Oh, come on," I said, feeling my face turning red. "Remember the first day of school—you both told some pretty tall stories. That's why I said that about the CIA, because I knew that working in a bank sounded pretty boring."

"Tall stories? What tall stories?" Lexie demanded.

"You know."

"No, I don't. Tell me."

"Well, Emily said that she lived on a ranch where they had horses two feet high. I mean, I know I'm a city girl, but give me a break. You expected me to believe that?"

"But it's true," Emily protested. "My mother breeds miniature horses. Our stallion is twenty-seven inches high, and some of our foals are only eighteen inches high. I'm not making it up, I swear. You can come see for yourself."

"There really are horses that small?"

"Honestly truly. Why do you think we call the ranch Thumbelina?"

"I didn't think about it," I said. "I just thought you were teasing me because I was a newcomer from the city."

"I wouldn't do that," Emily said. "I hate being teased, so why would I do it to anyone else?"

"And what tall story did you think I told you?" Lexie demanded.

She was looking at me so closely that I started blushing again. "About your parents," I said. "You know, you said your mother was a movie star. . . ."

"And?"

"She's not really a movie star, is she? You were making that up. I mean, you guys live in a condo."

"Okay, so maybe she's not a *big* movie star," Lexie said. "Not like Meryl Streep or Meg Ryan. But she's been in tons of movies. It's not her fault she doesn't get the top roles. She's very beautiful. She was in *Worlds Apart* last year. She played Raven's long-lost twin sister who stole the family fortune and went to Europe. That's why we lived down in L.A. for a long time."

"Oh." That's all I could think to say. Boy, did I feel stupid.

"And we live in a condo up here because then someone else takes care of the place when we're away," Lexie said. "It's a nice complex with a big pool. My mother likes it. It's safe and it's quiet and it's close enough for me to spend weekends with my dad."

". . . who really is a famous TV news cameraman?" I asked.

"Maybe not famous. Cameramen don't get to be famous," Lexie said, "but he gets to cover lots of exciting events. He flies all over the world, you know."

"And his arms never get tired," Emily quipped.

We looked at each other and started to smile.

"You must meet my dad. He's a lot of fun," Lexie said. "He says the most crazy things and makes me laugh."

"And you guys must come sleep over at our place and see the horses," Emily said. "We have some foals that are so sweet."

"Do you keep them in the house?" I asked.

"Are you kidding? They might be small, but they can still poop all over the floor," Emily said, laughing.

I lay back, feeling relaxed and contented. We'd been through a lot tonight, and we were like real friends now—comfortable with one another. Everything was going to be great, if only we could come up with a way to teach my brother a lesson he'd never forget.

I closed my eyes, trying to think, but my mind was blank. My stomach growled.

"I wish we hadn't had to throw away so much popcorn," Emily said. "There's nothing left and I'm starving."

"So am I," Lexie said.

"Do you want to go get some frozen yogurt and cookies?" I asked.

"I thought we could make another batch of popcorn," Lexie said with a wicked grin.

"And try two bags this time," Emily said.

We skipped down the stairs and into the kitchen. I rinsed the popcorn bowl and put it back in the cabinet.

"Wait, what's that noise?" Emily said suddenly. "There's somebody out there."

"Not again!"

"Didn't you hear it? Someone was moving around outside."

We all jumped a mile as the front door opened. Our nerves must have been completely frazzled— we'd forgotten my parents were due back now.

"Oh, hi, Mom. Hi, Dad. Welcome home," I said in a slightly shaky voice.

"What's the matter, girls?" my dad asked. "Is something wrong?"

"Wrong? No, nothing at all. Everything's fine," we all kind of said at the same time.

My mother was getting that suspicious look on her face.

"We came down for a snack," I said hastily. "How was your dinner?"

"Very nice, thank you," Mom said. "How was your evening? Did you have fun?"

"Oh yes, loads of fun," I said, at the same time that Emily said, "It was great!" and Lexie said, "We had a blast!"

"Well, that's good," my father said. "No problems at all? You didn't even set the house on fire?" He laughed as if that were a joke.

"Not even close," Lexie said.

My dad put his arm around Mom's shoulders. "See, honey, I said you were worrying about nothing."

"You were worrying, too," she said. "And what about Tom?" she asked us. "Did you see anything of him all evening?"

"Only a brief glimpse," I said.

My parents went across to the hall closet to hang up their coats. "I told you my lecture worked this time, Margaret," we heard my father say to my mother. He didn't think we could hear him. "The kid actually stayed in his room studying all evening. Maybe he's decided to shape up after all."

Emily and I looked at each other and smiled.

"He was prepared to work hard, because he really wanted to go on that bike ride tomorrow," Mom said. "What he needs is motivation, and then he'll do fine."

I couldn't stand there and listen to them a moment longer. I felt like bursting because I wanted to tell them what their precious son was really like and how their lectures and motivations really didn't work. If only I could have let them know the truth without getting myself into big trouble. There just had to be a way.

"I hope you girls are hungry," Dad asked.

"Haven't you been snacking all evening?" Mom said.

"Not at all. We had a drink of lemonade. That was it."

"That's very good of you. I'm pleasantly surprised," Mom said. "I thought eating too much was part of sleepovers."

"Not ours," Lexie said sweetly. "We had so many other things to do."

"Your father thought you might be hungry, so we brought you a treat," Mom said.

I noticed for the first time the white cardboard box in her hands.

"You did? What?"

"The rest of our dessert from the restaurant. Mr. Fisher ordered a huge piece of apple pie, but we were too full to eat, so he sent it home for you kids."

"Oh wow, great. I'll get out plates and forks," I said.

"And I'll put on the kettle for hot chocolate," Mom said.

"Do you think Tom might want to join you?" Dad asked.

I shook my head. "Tom? No, he's already asleep. He told us he was exhausted about an hour ago. He said he was going right to bed so he'd be ready for his bike ride in the morning. I wouldn't disturb him."

"Then we'll let sleeping dogs lie," Mom said.

"Good idea," I said, giving Lexie a triumphant smile.

ELEVEN

I woke to bright sunlight streaming in through my lacy curtains. Lexie was still asleep, curled in her sleeping bag with Barnaby Bunny in her arms. Asleep she looked quite different—sort of innocent and gentle, like a little child. I thought Emily was still asleep, too, but she was lying very still, staring at the ceiling.

"Emily, are you awake?" I whispered.

"Yes, I'm thinking."

"About our revenge on Tom?"

"Yes."

"Any good ideas yet?"

"Not yet."

"We have to hurry up. His friends are meeting him here for his big bike ride at nine thirty."

"We could reset his alarm so it doesn't wake him until ten," Emily suggested.

"My mother would only go up and wake him. She always notices the time."

Emily sat up. "It seems to me that he's always finding a way to put you down. Remember how he made fun of us in that biology lab when we got lost on the first day of school?"

"Yes," I said. "He always acts like he's so superior around me."

"So we have to find a way to make him look stupid," Emily said.

"Yes, but how?"

"Why are you guys making all this noise in the middle of the night?" Lexie groaned.

"It's not the middle of the night. It's almost nine in the morning," I said, "and we have to get moving if we want to find something to do to Tom before he leaves with his friends."

"Hasn't your great brain come up with a foolproof plan yet?"

"Not yet. Maybe we could do something to his bike."

Lexie got up, looking instantly wide awake. "Yeah, maybe we could hide the front wheel or mess up the brakes or something."

I shook my head. "That would just annoy him and convince him that I'm a brat. Plus it's dangerous. I want to teach him a lesson, not kill him. I just don't want him to bully me anymore."

Lexie was pulling on her sweats. "Let's go take a look. Maybe we'll come up with a brilliant idea when we see his bike."

"We could tell his friends that he's been grounded and he can't come on the bike ride after all," Emily suggested.

That wasn't bad. It was mean enough, but safe, and it would certainly make Tom very angry. But what if he told Mom about the horror movie?

110

"That has possibilities," I said. "Let's keep it in mind."

We all got dressed and went downstairs. There was nobody around except Christine. She was sitting in the kitchen in her silky robe, eating a big bowl of cereal.

"Hi," she called. "Want breakfast? I could whip you up some pancakes. Mom and Dad seem to be sleeping late."

"Pancakes would be great," I said. "But why are you up so early?" Usually she didn't show up until almost noon on weekends.

"School project," she said. "I got asked to help decorate the gym for the Welcome Dance tonight." She seemed to be in an unusually good mood, so I figured she had met a guy at the game or pizza place last night.

I remembered that Christine had left before Emily and Lexie had arrived for the sleepover. "Lexie and Emily, this is my sister, Christine," I said.

Everyone smiled at one another.

"Did you guys have fun last night?" Christine asked as she poured blueberries into the pancake mix.

I glanced across at Emily and Lexie. "We would have," I said, "except Tom played a mean joke on us."

"What did he do?"

I told her all about the horror movie and the zombie attack.

"We were trying to think of something to do to pay him back," Lexie said, "but we haven't come up with a good idea yet."

"I think we should scare him the way he scared us," Emily said.

"Good idea," Christine said. "What would scare Tom?"

"Pretending his bike was stolen?" Lexie suggested.

I shook my head. Tom loved that bike more than anything in the world. Even though I knew he deserved it, I couldn't be that mean to him.

"Does he sleep really heavily?" Emily asked.

"Like the dead," Christine said.

"Then we could put something scary in his room while he's asleep," Emily suggested.

"But what?" Lexie asked.

"He used to be scared of bugs," Christine said. "Remember, Kaitlin?"

My face lit up. "Yeah. He always freaked out watching some movie about ants crawling everywhere. And remember that time he wouldn't go to bed because there was a spider in his room?"

"So what do we do? Go outside and find ants?" Emily asked.

"I've got a fake spider from last Halloween," I said. "How about if we tie that over his bed?"

Lexie started jumping up and down. "How about if we build a giant spiderweb right over him and put the spider on it?"

"I have a good idea," Christine said. "I've got some of that fuzzy yarn left from the sweater I was knitting. You could start with that—"

"And we could dip it in pancake syrup first!" Emily shrieked, picking up the bottle.

We looked at each other in horrified delight.

Never in my life had I done anything so terrible and wonderful.

"Let's do it," I said.

Tom was invisible under his quilt as we crept into his room, carrying the sticky white yarn and the big hairy plastic spider. It was hard not to laugh as we started winding yarn from the head of his bed to the foot and back again. I was holding my breath every time one of us walked on a creaky floorboard, but Tom didn't even move. Soon a sticky spiderweb was strung from all four posters of Tom's bed. Then we put the big plastic spider right above where we thought Tom's face would be.

Emily picked up his alarm clock, checked her watch, and then set it to go off in one minute. We headed for the door and waited.

When the alarm clock rang, Tom stuck out an arm and hit the side of the web. He pulled off the covers and tried to sit up.

"Arghh!" he yelled as the sticky stuff brushed against his face and the spider landed on him. He thrashed about in a panic. "Get it off me! Mom, Dad! Help!"

Instead of Mom and Dad, Emily, Lexie, and I piled into his room.

"You're not scared of a plastic spider, are you, Tom?" I asked him. "That was so funny! I can't believe you fell for it."

We stood beside the bed, laughing crazily.

"I'm going to get you for this, you little creep,"

Tom growled at me, pulling the last strands of sticky yarn from his face. "You're dead meat."

"Kaitlin was only getting even with you for the mean tricks you played on us," Lexie said.

"What mean tricks? I only scared you guys a little last night."

"It wasn't just last night. You wouldn't help Kaitlin find a seat on the bus on Monday," Emily said. "Then you laughed at us in the biology lab when we were lost. And last night you scared us when we were already scared."

"I'd say you've been pretty mean to your sister, and so she's just getting even," Lexie said.

It felt good having friends on my side. "You know, I could have gone to Mom and Dad and told on you," I said. "But I didn't. And you would have gotten into much more trouble for sneaking out than I would have for watching a movie."

There was a long pause, and then Tom sighed.

"Maybe I was kind of mean and maybe you could have told Mom and Dad about last night. Okay, so you got me back and we're even. Now, will you help me get all this stuff off before Mom and Dad see it and so I can be ready to go on my bike ride?"

"I guess we did a good job, right?" Lexie asked.

"Humph," was all Tom said.

"I don't think you'll have any more trouble with him," Emily said as we washed the sticky stuff off our hands in the bathroom.

"I'd say we handled that pretty well," Lexie said. "We work great as a team."

"We sure do," I agreed. "I would never have gotten even with Tom without you two."

"The three musketeers," Emily said. "All for one and one for all! We'll sail through middle school as long as we're together."

She stood between me and Lexie, and we linked arms outside the bathroom and headed down the hall.

"We're going to have the greatest time—if we can just take care of Mr. Meany," Lexie said. "Next assignment for our great brains: we get even with Mr. Meany or die trying!"

With arms still linked we danced down the stairs. From the kitchen came the delicious smell of blueberry pancakes cooking.

Make your next party the best sleepover ever with these fabulous tips:

FUN FOOD

Every great sleepover begins with great snacks.

Frozen treats:
1) A day before the party fill an ice-cube tray with your favorite fruit juice
2) Cover the tray with plastic wrap
3) Stick a toothpick through the plastic, into each cube
4) Put the tray on an even surface in the freezer

By the time your party begins, they'll be delicious frozen treats!

Trail mix:
1) Mix together peanuts, or other nuts, and raisins in a bowl
2) For extra flavor add mini marshmallows, chocolate bits, and dried fruit

Ice-cream sundaes:

1) Ask each of your friends to bring one of the sundae ingredients (make sure you check with each other so you don't all bring the same thing!)

2) Ingredient List:
   - a) a jar of hot fudge
   - b) whipped cream
   - c) candy toppings
   - d) sprinkles
   - e) chopped nuts
   - f) and most importantly, ice cream!

3) Put each item on the kitchen counter or table

4) Set out napkins, spoons, and bowls for each person

5) Have an assembly line, so everyone can have a custom-made sundae

6) Dig in!

MOVIE MANIA

What would a sleepover be without a movie?

1) Check with your friends to see which movie they would like to see

2) Rent a movie from your local video store

3) Supplies you'll need:
   - a) tissues for a sad movie
   - b) blanket to hide under for a scary movie
   - c) popcorn, of course!

AT-HOME BEAUTY SALON

A little glamour can liven up any sleepover. Here are some ideas:

A Curly Do:
1) Wet your hair
2) Put in as many small braids as you can
3) Keep the braids in until the next morning and then take them out. You'll be surprised with your new kinky curly hair!

Make your own mini modeling shoot:
1) Gather the coolest outfits you can find
2) Ask your friends to bring clothes and jewelry
3) Get all dressed up as glamorously as you can
4) Take turns taking snapshots of each other
5) Develop pictures and share with your friends!

GAME TIME

Truth or Dare:
A sleepover is not a sleepover until you play Truth or Dare.
1) Write each person's name on a piece of paper and put it in a box
2) Everyone takes a turn at choosing a name from the box, and asking that person "Truth or dare?"
3) If the person chooses truth, she has to answer truthfully any (one) question you ask
4) If the person chooses dare, she has to follow

whatever dare you can think up (within reason—remember these are your friends).

Surprise Scenes:
Here's a role-playing game that's fun for a group!
1) Get two hats or bags
2) In one hat put names of settings (airplane, classroom, football game, the White House)
3) In the other hat put character types (librarian, grandmother, movie star, rock singer)
4) Pick two girls from the group
5) One girl picks a setting from the first hat
6) Each girl picks a character from the second hat
7) The two girls act out a scene pretending they are the characters in the place. It's sure to make you giggle!

ON THE CREATIVE SIDE ...

Dance Fever:
Dancing is a terrific thing to do at a sleepover.
1) Ask your friends to bring great tapes and CDs
2) Clear a space in a room and remove all breakable things
3) Put on music and dance away!
4) Make up your own dances and perform them for each other
5) Vote for best dancer of the night

Star Sleepover:

Have a sleepover where you and your friends are the stars. Here's how:

1) Decorate your walls with pictures of your favorite movie stars
2) Ask each friend to come dressed up as their favorite celebrity or TV show character
3) Have each girl stand up and imitate their character. The rest of the girls guess who he or she is
4) Vote for best impersonation

Crazy Collages:

1) You'll need:
   a) a stack of magazines
   b) cardboard or heavy paper
   c) newspaper
   d) a few pairs of scissors
   e) glue
   f) clear tape
   g) markers, paints, or colored pencils
   h) stickers, wrapping paper, colored paper, glitter, etc.
2) Spread out newspaper on a flat surface to keep work area clean
3) Cut fun pictures and words from magazines and paste onto the cardboard
4) Decorate them any way you want!

About the Author

Janet Quin-Harkin has written over fifty books for teenagers, including the best-seller *Ten-Boy Summer*. She is the author of the *Friends* series, the *Heartbreak Café* series, the *Senior Year* series, and *The Boyfriend Club* series. She has also written several romances.

Ms. Quin-Harkin lives with her husband in San Rafael, California. She has four children. In addition to writing books, she teaches creative writing at a nearby college.